YES MINISTER

To Yvon
From The Section.
Congratulations !

Glaze 3hr/1b.
last 15 min.
breast from
royal jam
ginger - shredded
tabasco.

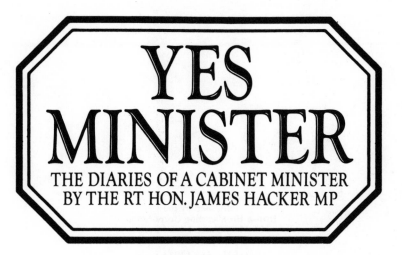

YES MINISTER

THE DIARIES OF A CABINET MINISTER
BY THE RT HON. JAMES HACKER MP

Volume One

Edited by Jonathan Lynn
and Antony Jay

BRITISH BROADCASTING CORPORATION

Published by the
British Broadcasting Corporation
35 Marylebone High Street
London W1M 4AA

ISBN 0 563 17934 1
First published 1981
Reprinted 1981 1983

Printed in England
by Mackays of Chatham Ltd

Contents

Editors' Note

Some note of explanation is needed on the methods and guidelines we have used in reducing a diary of many millions of words to one relatively short volume.

Our main purpose has been to simplify and therefore clarify. Although this was also Hacker's intention, years of political training and experience had taught him to use twenty words where one would do, to write millions of words where mere thousands would suffice, to use language to blur and fudge the issues and events so that they become incomprehensible to others. When incomprehensibility has been achieved by a politician, so has temporary safety.

Nonetheless, we believe that Hacker wrote these diaries, a unique contribution to our understanding of the way Britain was governed in the 1980s, in the hope that the people would understand more, not less. So we have edited them ruthlessly.

This first volume covers Hacker's initial experience in government, as Minister for Administrative Affairs. This Ministry had been created some years earlier as an umbrella Ministry, along the lines of George Brown's Department of Economic Affairs in the Wilson government of the sixties, to coordinate government administration. Theoretically it gave Hacker a roving brief, to investigate and control administrative inefficiency and overspending throughout the system, wherever it was to be found. Unfortunately, however, the Department of Administrative Affairs was not only created to control the Civil Service, it had to be staffed by the Civil Service. Readers may therefore guess the inevitable results of Hacker's labours.

It remains a slight puzzle to us that Hacker, who was such a master of blurring and obfuscation in his own political dealings, should have been so unable to deal with a group of civil servants whose techniques were essentially similar. Hacker's innocence, as revealed in these diaries, is quite touching.

Later volumes, which we are still editing, deal with the rest of Hacker's career at the Department of Administrative Affairs, and continue as he failed upwards from one senior cabinet post to the next, culminating with his ultimate failure at Number Ten and his final demise on his elevation to the House of Lords (as it then was).

There was no single overriding principle by which we decided what to cut and what to retain. Broadly, we tried to preserve the narrative element of the original diary. Thus, we have tended to pursue particular stories and trains of events to their conclusion, rather than deal with events in their original random chronological sequence.

Hacker was, inevitably, in ignorance of certain conversations and events which, had he known of them, would have doubtless changed his perception and his views. We are fortunate that under the so-called '30-year rule' all of Sir Humphrey Appleby's memos and minutes have become available to us.

We are also fortunate that, because Sir Humphrey Appleby was in every way the perfect civil servant, he had a total belief in the value of paperwork and committed *everything* to paper in one form or another. Therefore we have had the benefit not only of DAA memos but also of Sir Humphrey's own private diaries.

We are also most grateful to have had a few conversations with Sir Humphrey himself before the advancing years, without in any way impairing his verbal fluency, disengaged the operation of his mind from the content of his speech. We are also grateful for many useful conversations with Sir Bernard Woolley GCB, former Head of the Civil Service, who was Hacker's Private Secretary at the time this section of Diaries was written.

Jonathan Lynn
Antony Jay
Hacker College, Oxford.
July, 2017 AD

1
Open Government

October 22nd

Well, perhaps it's the early hours of Friday, the 23rd now. I am most excited. I have just been returned to Parliament by Birmingham East. And after years in opposition, the party has finally won a general election and we're back in office.

After the result was announced I went to the celebration do at Alderman Spotteswood's[1] and saw Robert McKenzie on the telly say: 'And so Jim Hacker's back, with an increased majority in his marginal constituency. After many years as a Shadow Minister he seems almost certain to get a Cabinet post in the new government.'

Robin Day seemed doubtful, though. I do hope Bob McKenzie's right.

October 23rd

I'm still hoping but I wonder if Robin Day knows something that I don't.

I've been sitting by the telephone ever since breakfast. No potential Cabinet Minister ever moves more than twenty feet from the telephone in the twenty-four hours following the appointment of a new Prime Minister. If you haven't heard within twenty-four hours, you're not going to be in the Cabinet.

Annie kept me supplied with constant cups of coffee all morning, and when I returned to the armchair next to the phone after lunch she asked me to help do the Brussels sprouts for dinner if I didn't have anything else to do. I explained to her that I couldn't because I was waiting for the call.

'Who from?' Sometimes Annie really is a bit dense.

The phone rang. I grabbed it. It was Frank Weisel, my special

---

[1] Hacker's constituency party Chairman.

political adviser, saying that he was on his way over. I told Annie, who wasn't pleased.

'Why doesn't he just move in?' she asked bitterly.

Sometimes I just don't understand her. I patiently explained to her that, as my political adviser, I depend on Frank more than anyone. 'Then why don't you marry *him*?' she asked. 'I now pronounce you man and political adviser. Whom politics has joined let no wife put asunder.'

It is awfully difficult for Annie, I know. Being an MP's wife is a pretty thankless task. But now that I may be a Minister, she'll at last reap the rewards!

The phone rang all day. Alderman Spotteswoode, the Gas Board, Frank, all sorts of useless people ringing up to congratulate me. 'On what?' I said to Annie: 'Don't they realise I'm waiting for the call?'

She said, 'You sound as if you're about to enter the ministry.'

'Yes,' I said, 'but which ministry, that's the whole point.'

Suddenly Annie screamed. I couldn't believe my ears. 'It was a *joke*!' she shouted, and started to pull her hair out. I decided that she must be a bit tense.

'Are you a bit tense?' I asked. She screamed again, and threw herself onto the floor. I thought of calling an ambulance, but was worried about the adverse publicity affecting my career at this crucial juncture – NEW MINISTER'S WIFE TAKEN AWAY IN STRAIT-JACKET.

'Are you a bit tense?' I asked again. Carefully.

'No,' she shouted – 'No, no, no, I'm not tense. I'm just a politician's wife. I'm not allowed to have feelings. I'm just a happy carefree politician's wife.'

So I asked her why she was lying face downwards on the floor. 'I'm looking for a cigarette. I can't find any.'

'Try the cigarette box,' I advised, trying to keep calm.

'It's empty.'

'Take a valium.'

'I can't find the valium, that's why I'm looking for a cigarette. Jim, pop out and get me some.'

I explained to Annie that I simply didn't dare leave the phone. Annie betrayed her usual total lack of understanding. 'Look, if the PM wants you to be in the bloody Cabinet, the PM will phone back if you're out. Or you can phone back.'

Annie will never understand the finer points of politics.

[*Hacker was very insecure about his cabinet prospects because he had previously run Martin Walker's campaign against the new PM for*

10

the leadership of the party. The question was whether the PM would be strong enough to ignore Jim Hacker or whether, in the interests of party unity, the PM would be obliged to give him a good job – Ed.]

By the end of today I've heard on the grapevine that Bill's got Europe. Poor old Europe. Bill can't speak French or German. He hardly even speaks English, as a matter of fact. Martin's got the Foreign Office, as expected, Jack's got Health and Fred's got Energy.

I told Annie of these appointments, and she asked me if anyone had got Brains? I suppose she means Education.

October 24th
At last I'm a Cabinet Minister.

And today I had my first encounter with the Civil Service, and I must say I am very impressed.

I got the call from Number Ten at about 9 a.m., after a sleepless night, and immediately Frank Weisel and I caught the London train. I got a taxi to Number Ten, where I was asked by the PM to take over the Department of Administrative Affairs.

This is an important post. In the Cabinet ranking, about eighth or ninth I should think. On the other hand, Martin reminded me (when he phoned to congratulate me) that the DAA is a political graveyard, a bit like the Home Office, and the PM may have over-promoted me – a vengeful move. I am determined to get a grip on the DAA and prove to the PM that I'm not so easily taken care of.

I was expecting to be Minister of Agriculture, as I've shadowed Agriculture for seven years, and have many good ideas about it, but for some inexplicable reason the PM decided against this.

[*We found a memo from Sir Andrew Donnelly, Permanent Secretary of Agriculture, to Sir Arnold Robinson, Secretary to the Cabinet, imploring Sir Arnold to make sure that Hacker did not get Agriculture as he was too 'genned up' on it. Cabinet Papers show that Sir Arnold managed to convey to the PM that it would be better for Hacker not to go to Agriculture because 'he's been thinking about it rather too long and is perhaps in a bit of a rut' – Ed.*]

An official car met me as I came out of Number Ten, and I was driven straight to the DAA. I was met on the front steps by Bernard Woolley, who is to be my Private Secretary, and his assistant. He seems a likeable enough chap.

To my surprise he instantly knew who Frank Weisel was, as we got out of the car, though he pronounced his name 'Weasel', which always infuriates Frank.

We walked down miles of corridors. When we got to my office Frank had disappeared with the Assistant Private Secretary. Bernard assured me that Frank was being taken care of. They really are awfully nice and helpful.

My office is large, with a big desk, a conference table with lots of chairs around it, and a few armchairs arranged around a coffee table to form a conversation area. Otherwise, rather characterless. Bernard immediately went to the drinks cupboard.

'A drink, Minister?'

I nodded. 'Jim,' I said, as I want us to be on first name terms.

'Gin?' he said, mishearing me.

'No,' I said, 'Jim. Call me Jim.'

Bernard said: 'If it's all the same to you, I'd rather call you Minister, Minister.'

'Minister, Minister?' It reminded me of Major Major in *Catch-22*. Then I realised what he meant. I asked him, 'Does that mean I have to call you Private Secretary, Private Secretary?'

Bernard said I was to call him Bernard. I'm sure that in the course of time I'll persuade him to call me Jim.

A moment later Sir Humphrey Appleby arrived. He is the Permanent Secretary of the DAA, the Civil Service Head of the Department. He is in his early fifties I should think, but – somehow – ageless. He is charming and intelligent, a typical mandarin. He welcomed me to the Department.

'I believe you've met before,' Bernard remarked. I was struck for the second time how well-informed this young man is.

Sir Humphrey said, 'Yes, we did cross swords when the Minister gave me a grilling over the Estimates in the Public Accounts Committee last year. He asked me all the questions I hoped nobody would ask.'

This is splendid. Sir Humphrey clearly admires me. I tried to brush it off. 'Well,' I said, 'Opposition's about asking awkward questions.'

'Yes,' said Sir Humphrey, 'and government is about not answering them.'

I was surprised. 'But you answered all my questions, didn't you,' I commented.

'I'm glad you thought so, Minister,' said Sir Humphrey. I didn't quite know what he meant by that. I decided to ask him who else was in the department.

'Briefly, sir, I am the Permanent Under-Secretary of State, known as the Permanent Secretary. Woolley here is your Principal Private

Secretary. I, too, have a Principal Private Secretary, and he is the Principal Private Secretary to the Permanent Secretary. Directly responsible to me are ten Deputy Secretaries, eighty-seven Under-Secretaries and two hundred and nineteen Assistant Secretaries. Directly responsible to the Principal Private Secretaries are plain Private Secretaries. The Prime Minister will be appointing two Parliamentary Under Secretaries and you will be appointing your own Parliamentary Private Secretary.'

'Can they all type?' I joked.

'None of us can type, Minister,' replied Sir Humphrey smoothly. 'Mrs McKay types – she is your secretary.'

I couldn't tell whether or not he was joking. 'What a pity,' I said. 'We could have opened an agency.'

Sir Humphrey and Bernard laughed. 'Very droll, sir,' said Sir Humphrey. 'Most amusing, sir,' said Bernard. Were they genuinely amused at my wit, or just being rather patronising? 'I suppose they all say that, do they?' I ventured.

Sir Humphrey reassured me on that. 'Certainly not, Minister,' he replied. 'Not quite all.'

I decided to take charge at once. I sat behind my desk and to my dismay I found it had a swivel chair. I don't like swivel chairs. But Bernard immediately assured me that everything in the office can be changed at my command – furniture, decor, paintings, office routine. I am unquestionably the boss!

Bernard then told me that they have two types of chair in stock, to go with two kinds of Minister – 'One sort folds up instantly and the other sort goes round and round in circles.' On second thoughts, perhaps that was another of Bernard's little jokes.

I decided that the time had come to be blunt and to tell them what's what. 'Frankly,' I said, 'this Department has got to cut a great swathe through the whole of the stuffy Whitehall bureaucracy. We need a new broom. We are going to throw open the windows and let in a bit of fresh air. We are going to cut through the red tape and streamline this creaking old bureaucratic machine. We are going to have a clean sweep. There are far too many useless people just sitting behind desks.'

I became aware that *I* was actually sitting behind a desk, but I'm sure that they realised that I was not referring to myself.

I explained that we had to start by getting rid of people who just make work for each other. Sir Humphrey was very helpful, and suggested that I mean re-deploy them – which, I suppose, is what I *do*

13

mean. I certainly want to reduce overmanning, but I don't actually want to be responsible for putting people out of work.

But, by the clean sweep and the new broom, I mean that we must have more Open Government. We made election pledges about this, and I intend to keep them. We must take the nation into our confidence. I said all this to Humphrey and Bernard who, to my surprise, were wholeheartedly in favour of these ideas.

Humphrey referred to my speeches on this subject in the House last year. And he referred to my *Observer* article, *Daily Mail* interview, and the manifesto.

I am most impressed that he knows so much about me.

Humphrey then produced draft proposals, to implement my policy in a White Paper. I was flabbergasted. The efficiency of the Civil Service is quite astounding. They even plan, Sir Humphrey tells me, to call the White Paper 'Open Government.'

All of these draft proposals are available to me within thirty-six hours of the new government being elected and within minutes of my arrival at my office. And on a weekend! Remarkable chaps. I asked Humphrey who had done all this.

'The creaking old bureaucratic machine,' he replied with a smile. 'No seriously, Minister, we are fully seized of the need for reform and we have taken it on board.'

I told him I was slightly surprised.

'I thought I'd have to fight you all the way,' I said.

Sir Humphrey remarked that people have funny ideas about the Civil Service.

'We are just here to help you formulate and implement your policies,' he explained.

He seems most sincere.

The draft proposals, which I have brought home tonight to my London flat in a red box, include 'Proposals for Shortening Approval Procedures in Planning Appeals.' Excellent. Sir Humphrey was able to quote my rather amusing question in the House, which I'd asked earlier this year, from *Hansard*:

Mr. James Hacker (Birmingham, East): Is the Minister aware that planning procedures make building a bungalow in the Twentieth Century slower than building a cathedral in the Twelfth Century? Opposition laughter, and government cries of "shame".

[Actually they cried 'Bollocks' – Ed.]

As it's Saturday, we have arranged to start things properly on Monday morning. But they've given me six red boxes for the weekend, four to be completed by tonight and two more tomorrow. Bernard tells me that the previous Minister got a bit slack about the paperwork, especially during the election campaign.

I'm certainly not going to be slack! I shall read everything they give me to read.

October 26th

I read all my boxes over the weekend. It took about nine hours. I caught the 7.15 a.m. train to Euston, the official car met me, and I was in the office by 9.20.

All the draft proposals for Open Government are superficially pretty impressive, but I happen to know that the Civil Service is pretty good at delaying tactics. I mentioned this to Humphrey at a meeting today. I think he's getting to know who's boss around here.

But first things first. The day started with the diary. I found to my surprise that there were numerous appointments in it already. I asked how this was possible, since they didn't even know who would win the election.

Bernard said: 'We knew there'd be a Minister, Minister.' I told him not to start *that* again.

Sir Humphrey explained, 'Her Majesty likes the business of government to continue, even when there are no politicians around.'

'Isn't that very difficult?' I asked.

'Yes . . . and no,' said Humphrey. I must say, I can't see how it's possible to govern without the politicians. I'm afraid that Humphrey might have delusions of grandeur . . .

My diary was pretty frightening. Cabinet at 10.00 on Thursday. Nine Cabinet committees this week. A speech to the Law Institute tomorrow night, a deputation from the British Computer Association at 10.30 tomorrow morning, University Vice-Chancellors lunch on Wednesday (another speech), opening the National Conference of Public Employers on Thursday morning (another speech), and so on.

I noticed that everything in the diary is in pencil, so presumably much of it can be and will be changed. I pointed out to Bernard that I have various other commitments.

Bernard looked puzzled. 'Such as?' he asked.

'Well . . . I'm on four policy committees of the party, for a start.'

'I'm sure you won't be wanting to put party before country,' said Sir Humphrey. I had never looked at it in that light. Of course, he's absolutely right.

They were going to give me three more red boxes for tonight, by the way. When I jibbed at this a bit, Sir Humphrey explained that there are a lot of decisions to take and announcements to approve. He then tried something on, by saying: 'But we could, in fact, minimise the work so that you need only take the major policy decisions.'

I saw through that ploy at once. I insisted that *I* would take *all* the decisions and read *all* the relevant documents.

They've given me five boxes for tonight.

October 27th

Today I found that we have a problem with Frank Weisel. It's Tuesday today, and I realised that I hadn't seen him since I arrived at the DAA last Saturday morning.

To be quite truthful, I didn't actually realise it till he barged into my office, shouting and carrying on, demanding to be let in.

It appears that he's been in the waiting room since Saturday. (I presume he went home on Sunday.) Bernard tried to tell him that he, Humphrey and I were in private conference, but I quickly sorted that out. I demanded that Frank, as my adviser, be given an office in the Department.

Sir Humphrey attempted to fudge the issue, saying that I had a whole Department to advise me now. Nonetheless I insisted.

'Well,' said Sir Humphrey, 'I believe we have some spare office space in Walthamstow, don't we Bernard?'

Frank was appalled. 'Walthamstow?'

'Yes, it's surprising isn't it?' said Sir Humphrey agreeably. 'The government owns property all over London.'

'But I don't want to be in Walthamstow,' explained Frank at the top of his voice.

'It's in a very nice part of Walthamstow,' put in Bernard.

16

'And Walthamstow's a very nice place. So I gather,' added Sir Humphrey.

Frank and I looked at each other. If they were not so charming and, well, gentlemanly, you might have thought they were trying to squeeze Frank right out.

'I need an office *here*, in this building,' said Frank, firmly and extremely loudly.

I added my agreement. Sir Humphrey capitulated at once, and told Bernard to find a suitable office right away. I then said, to make assurance doubly sure, that I expected Frank to have copies of all the papers that are given to me.

Bernard seemed surprised. 'All?'

'All,' I said.

Sir Humphrey agreed immediately. 'It shall be done – all the appropriate papers.'

In my opinion, these civil servants are not nearly so hard to deal with as people say. They are mostly very co-operative, and, even if not initially, always jump to it when spoken to firmly. I think I'm getting somewhere at last.

October 28th

After the last hectic four days, I have a little time to reflect – for posterity – on my first days in office.

First, I am impressed by the thorough grasp the officials at the DAA have of every situation. Second, how they are willing to co-operate fully, albeit under pressure, with Frank Weisel.

Thirdly, I am most struck by my dependence on these civil servants. I, like virtually all our new administration, knew nothing of the workings of Whitehall except what I'd learned secondhand. Because we have been so long in opposition, only three members of the government, including the PM, have ever held office before. I had never seen the inside of a red box, never met a Permanent Secretary, and had no idea how things were really done. [*This situation is similar to the one in which the Labour Government of 1964 found itself – Harold Wilson, the PM, was the only member of Cabinet who had previously been a Cabinet Minister – Ed.*] This makes us more dependent on our officials than most new governments. Thank goodness they are behaving honourably.

[*The following Monday, Sir Humphrey Appleby met Sir Arnold Robinson, Secretary to the Cabinet, at The Reform Club in Pall Mall. Sir Humphrey made a note about the meeting in his private diary.*]

November 2 MONDAY

Arnold and I compared
notes about the new government. His new Cabinet is
scarcely distinguishable from
the last one. My new boy is
learning the rules very quickly.

I sounded Arnold out about
the American Ambassador -
rumour has it he has been
spending a lot of time
with the PM.

[*It is interesting to observe that senior civil servants, perhaps because they have spent thirty years writing notes in the margin of a memo or minute, only write in the margin even if there is nothing else on the page – Ed.*]

Arnold and I compared notes [on November 2] about the new government. His new Cabinet is scarcely distinguishable from the last one. My new boy is learning the rules very quickly.

I sounded Arnold out about the American Ambassador – rumour has it he has been spending a lot of time with the PM.

Arnold confirmed this. But was unwilling to say whether it was about defence or trade. He is anxious about a leak – therefore it is imperative that the Cabinet doesn't hear about it yet.

I concluded, correctly, that it is defence *and* trade i.e. the new aerospace systems contract.

The aerospace contract would be a considerable coup for the PM, less than two weeks after the election. Of course, it's been in the pipeline for months, but the new PM will obviously take the credit.

It will mean four and a half billion dollars, and many new jobs in the Midlands and North-West. All in marginal seats, too – what a coincidence!

This is valuable information. I gathered from Arnold that it would, therefore, be a grave embarrassment to the PM if a hypothetical Minister were to rock the Anglo-American boat. Man overboard. The end of a promising new Ministerial career, in fact.

Therefore, I have ensured that the Weasel[1] receives a copy of the invoice

[1] Frank Weisel.

18

for the new American addressing machines. Naturally he has not received it, because it is sensitive. But I think that this is the right moment.

I instructed my secretary to ensure that the Weasel find the invoice near the bottom of a pile. Let the man feel he has achieved something.

[*Bernard Woolley joined Sir Humphrey and Sir Arnold at the club, for an after-dinner coffee while they drank their after-dinner brandy – Ed.*]

I asked young Bernard what he makes of our new Minister. Bernard is happy. So am I. Hacker swallowed the whole diary in one gulp and apparently did his boxes like a lamb last Saturday and Sunday. He'll be house-trained in no time.

All we have to do is head him off this Open Government nonsense, I remarked to Bernard. Bernard said that he thought that we were in favour of Open Government. I hope I have not over-promoted young Bernard. He still has an awful lot to learn.

I explained that we are calling the White Paper *Open Government* because you always dispose of the difficult bit in the title. It does less harm there than on the statute books.

It is the law of Inverse Relevance: the less you intend to do about something, the more you have to keep talking about it.

Bernard asked us, 'What's wrong with Open Government?' I could hardly believe my ears. Arnold thought he was joking. Sometimes I wonder if Bernard really is a flyer, or whether we shouldn't just send him off to a career at the War Graves Commission.

Arnold pointed out, with great clarity, that Open Government is a contradiction in terms. You can be open – or you can have government.

Bernard claims that the citizens of a democracy have a right to know. We explained that, in fact, they have a right to be ignorant. Knowledge only means complicity and guilt. Ignorance has a certain dignity.

Bernard then said: 'The Minister wants Open Government'. Years of training seem to have had no effect on Bernard sometimes.

I remarked that one does not just give people what they want, if it's not good for them. One does not, for instance, give whisky to an alcoholic.

Arnold rightly added that if people do not know what you're doing, they don't know what you're doing *wrong*.

This is not just a defence mechanism for officials, of course. Bernard must understand that he would not be serving his Minister by helping him to make a fool of himself. Every Minister we have would have been a laughing stock within his first three weeks in office if it had not been for the most rigid and impenetrable secrecy about what he was up to.

Bernard is a Private Secretary. I am a Permanent Under-Secretary of State. The very word Secretary means one who can keep a secret.

Bernard asked me what I proposed to do. Naturally I did not inform him of my plans for the Weasel to make a great discovery. This would be putting too great a strain on Bernard's loyalty to Hacker.

19

I asked Bernard if he could keep a secret. He said he could. I replied that *I* could, too. [*Appleby Papers 14/QLI/9a*]

[*Hacker was, of course, in complete ignorance of the meeting described above – Ed.*]

November 5th

Guy Fawkes day. Fireworks inside the office too. A fitting day on which to enforce the supremacy of parliament and HMG.

Frank Weisel came bursting into my office, waving a document, 'Have you seen this?' he enquired at four thousand decibels.

I was delighted that the civil servants were giving him all the papers now. I said so.

'They're not,' he said derisively. 'Not the *real* papers.'

'Which real papers aren't you getting?' I wanted to know.

'How do I know, if I'm not getting them?'

This is, of course, absolutely true. And I don't know what he can do about it. [*This, of course, is an example of what management consultants call the Light-in-the-Refrigerator Syndrome i.e. is the light on when the door is shut? The only way to find out is to open the door – in which case the door is not shut any more – Ed.*]

But Frank did not want to discuss his problems in getting necessary information out of the officials.

'They think they're sending me the rubbish. But look what I've found – Oho, we've got them, we've got them by the short and curlies.'

I still didn't know what he was talking about. Frank explained further.

'We've got Sir Humphrey-Bloody-Appleby and Mr Toffee-Nose-Private-Secretary-Snooty-Woolley just where we want them.'

He brandished a sheaf of papers under my nose. I *still* didn't know what he was talking about, but I do think he has a wonderful line in invective – perhaps I should let him write the draft of my conference speech next year.

I made Frank sit down, and explain calmly. He has found some ordinary office invoices that have tremendous political significance. The DAA has apparently bought one thousand computer video display terminals, at ten thousand pounds each. Ten million pounds of the taxpayers' money. And they are made in Pittsburgh!

This is shocking. Humphrey's been keeping very quiet about this. And I'm not surprised. We make computer peripherals in my constituency, Birmingham East. And we have rising unemployment. It is a scandal that the Civil Service is not buying British.

I sent for Humphrey. He was in meetings all day, but Frank and I will confront him with this tomorrow. I am deeply grateful to Frank. Sir Humphrey is going to be very surprised indeed that we have found out about this so fast.

November 6th

The meeting with Humphrey was a total success.

I showed him the invoices for the computer display terminals. He admitted that the DAA has purchased this brand for the whole of Whitehall.

'But they're not British,' I pointed out.

'That is unfortunately true,' he agreed, somewhat shamefaced.

'We make these machines in Birmingham East.'

'Not of the same quality,' he said.

This is very probably true, but naturally I can't admit it even if it is.

'They are better quality,' I said firmly. 'They come from my constituency.' I told Humphrey to cancel the contract.

He responded that it was beyond his power to do so, and that it could only be cancelled by the Treasury. He said it would be a major change of policy for the Civil Service to cancel contracts freely entered into. Especially with overseas suppliers.

He suggested (a trifle impertinently, I thought) that I should take it up in Cabinet. 'Perhaps they would postpone the discussion on the Middle East, or nuclear disarmament, to talk about office equipment.'

I could see that this was out of the question. I was faced with a dilemma. If it couldn't be cancelled, how was I to face my constituency party?

'Why need they know?' asked Sir Humphrey. 'Why need *anybody* know? We can see that it never gets out.'

I was staggered. Couldn't Humphrey see that to keep it quiet was directly contrary to our new policy of Open Government, to which he was as firmly committed as I?

Frank spelled out the only alternative. 'If the order can't be cancelled, it must be published.'

Humphrey asked why. For a moment I couldn't quite think of the answer. But Frank saw it at once. 'Two reasons,' he explained. 'First, it's a manifesto commitment. Second, it'll make the last Minister look like a traitor.'

Two unanswerable reasons. I really am very grateful to Frank. And he is running rings around Sir Humphrey. Perhaps Sir Humphrey is not as clever as I first thought.

Humphrey seemed very anxious about the idea of publication. 'But surely,' he said to Frank, 'you're not suggesting that the Minister should make a positive reference to this confidential transaction in a speech?'

'A speech!' said Frank. 'Of course! That's the answer.'

This is a superb idea of Frank's. My speech to the Union of Office Employees will deal with this scandalous contract. And we will release it to the Press in advance.

I said as much to Humphrey. Frank said, 'There. Who's running the country now?' I felt his glee was a little juvenile, but quite understandable.

Sir Humphrey seemed even more worried. I asked him for his advice, which was totally predictable. 'I think it might be regrettable if we upset the Americans.'

Predictable, and laughable. I pointed out to Humphrey, in no uncertain terms, that it is high time that someone jolted the Americans out of their commercial complacency. We should be thinking about the British poor, not the American rich!

Humphrey said, 'Minister, if that is your express wish the Department will back you. Up to the hilt.' This was very loyal. One must give credit where it's due.

I said that indeed it was my express wish. Bernard then said he would circulate the speech, as soon as it was written, for clearance.

This is new to me. I've never heard of 'clearance'. More bureaucracy and pointless paperwork. This matter has nothing to do with any other department. And if another department disagrees, they can say so publicly. That's what Open Government is all about.

Humphrey pleaded with me to circulate the speech, if only for information. At first I opposed this, but he argued – quite convincingly, I thought – that Open Government demands that we should inform our colleagues in government as well as our friends in Fleet Street.

My final word to Humphrey, as the meeting concluded, was to see that the speech went straight to the Press.

'Minister,' he said, 'we shall obviously serve your best interests.'

A notable victory by Frank and me, in the cause of Open Government.

[*A typescript of Hacker's speech has been found in the files of the DAA. It is annotated with suggestions by Frank Weisel and Bernard Woolley, with comments from Hacker – Ed.*]

DEPARTMENT OF
ADMINISTRATIVE AFFAIRS

SPEECH TO THE UNION OF OFFICE EMPLOYEES

As you know, we have made a pledge to the
people about Open Government.   So let's begin
as we mean to go on.   The people have a right
to know what I know.   And I have discovered
that only last month the previous government
signed a contract to import ten million
pounds worth of office equipment from America
for use by the Service.

Civil Service bureaucrat? Frank

YES. GOOD! J.H

And yet an identical product – a better
product – is made in Britain.   By British
workers.   In British factories.   So we are
being fobbed off with second-rate American
junk by high-pressure smart-alec salesmen
from Pittsburgh while British factories
stand idle and British workers queue up for
the dole.

Unemployment benefit? B.W.

DOLE! J.H

Well, if the Americans are going to take us
for a ride, at least the British people have
a right to know about it.   And we will fight
them on the beaches, we will fight them

/over

November 8th

Today was disastrous. There have been some quite astounding turns of events.

My speech was completed. I was sitting in the office reading the Press Release when Bernard burst in with a minute from the PM's private office.

I have learned, by the way, that *minutes, memos* and *submissions* are all the same thing. Except that ministers send *minutes* to civil servants and to each other, whereas civil servants send *memos* and *minutes* to each other but *submissions* to ministers.

[*This is because a minute takes or orders action whereas a memo presents the background arguments, the pros and cons. Therefore, civil servants may send either to each other, as may politicians – but as a civil servant may not tell a Minister what to do he sends a submission, the very word designed to express an attitude of humility and respect. Minutes may, of course, also be notes about official meetings, and this meaning gives rise to the well-known civil service axiom that meetings are where civil servants take minutes but politicians take hours. – Ed.*]

Anyway, the minute made it clear that we were all to be very nice to the Yanks for the next few weeks. I realised that my speech, which had gone out to the press, could not have been timed worse.

I was appalled. Not only by my bad luck. But I find it incredible that I, as a member of the Cabinet, should have no knowledge of forthcoming defence agreements with the Americans. Whatever has happened to the doctrine of collective responsibility that I learned about at the LSE?

10 DOWNING STREET

November 7th

TO ALL DEPARTMENTS

To inform you that the Prime Minister is planning a visit to Washington next month, and is anxious that the visit will result in a valuable Anglo-American defence trade agreement. The importance of this agreement cannot be overestimated.

Sir Humphrey then hurried in to my office, looking slightly panicky.

'Sorry to burst in Minister, but all hell's broken loose at Number Ten – apparently they've just seen your speech. They are asking why we didn't obtain clearance.'

'What did you say?' I asked.

'I said that we believe in Open Government. But it seemed to make things worse. The PM wants to see you in the House, right away.'

I realised that this could be the end for me. I asked Humphrey what was likely to happen. Sir Humphrey shrugged.

'The Prime Minister giveth – and the Prime Minister taketh away.'

I left the room feeling sick. As I started down the corridor I thought I heard Sir Humphrey add: 'Blessed be the name of the Prime Minister.' But I think I must have imagined that.

Humphrey, Frank and I hurried down Whitehall past the Cenotaph (how very appropriate that seemed!). There was an icy wind blowing. We went straight to the House. I was to meet the PM behind the Speaker's chair.

[*This does not mean, literally, behind the chair. It is the area of the House where the PM and the Leader of the Opposition, the two Chief Whips, the Leader of the House and others, meet on neutral ground to arrange the business of the House. The PM's office is to be found there too. – Ed.*]

We were kept waiting for some minutes outside the PM's room. Then Vic Gould, our Chief Whip, emerged. He came straight over to me.

'You're a real pain in the arse, aren't you?' Vic really does pride himself on his dreadful manners. 'The PM's going up the wall. Hitting the roof. You can't go around making speeches like that.'

'It's Open Government,' said Frank.

'Shut up, Weasel, who asked you?' retorted Vic. Rude bugger. Typical Chief Whip.

'Weisel,' said Frank with dignity.

I sprang to Frank's defence. 'He's right, Vic. It's Open Government. It's in our manifesto. One of our main planks. The PM believes in Open Government too.'

'Open, yes,' said Vic. 'But not gaping.' Very witty, I don't think! 'In politics,' Vic went on relentlessly, 'you've got to learn to say things with tact and finesse – you berk!'

I suppose he's got a point. I felt very sheepish, but partly because I didn't exactly enjoy being ignominiously ticked off in front of Humphrey and Frank.

'How long have you been a Minister?' Vic asked me. Bloody silly question. He knows perfectly well. He was just asking for effect.

'A week and a half,' I told him.

'Then I think you may have earned yourself a place in the *Guinness Book of Records*,' he replied. 'I can see the headlines already – CABINET SPLIT ON U.S. TRADE. HACKER LEADS REVOLT AGAINST PRIME MINISTER! That's what you wanted, is it?'

And he walked away.

Then Sir Arnold Robinson, the Cabinet Secretary, came out of the PM's office. Sir Humphrey asked him what news there was.

Sir Arnold said the same things, only in Whitehall language. 'That speech is causing the Prime Minister some distress. Has it definitely been released to the Press?'

I explained that I gave express instructions for it to go out at twelve noon. Sir Arnold seemed angry with Sir Humphrey. 'I'm appalled at you,' he said. I've never heard one civil servant express himself so strongly to another. 'How could you allow your Minister to put himself in this position without going through the proper channels?'

Humphrey turned to me for help. 'The Minister and I,' he began, 'believe in Open Government. We want to throw open the windows and let in a bit of fresh air. Isn't that right, Minister?'

I nodded, but couldn't speak. For the first time, Sir Arnold addressed me directly.

'Well, Minister, it's good party stuff but it places the PM in a very difficult position, personally.' That, in Sir Arnold's language, is about the most threatening thing that has ever been said to me.

'But . . . what about our commitment to Open Government?' I finally managed to ask.

'This,' replied Sir Arnold drily, 'seems to be the closed season for Open Government.'

Then Sir Humphrey voiced my worst fears by murmuring quietly: 'Do you want to give thought to a draft letter of resignation? Just in case, of course.'

I know that Humphrey was just trying to be helpful, but he really doesn't give much moral support in a crisis.

I could see that there was only one possibility left. 'Can't we hush it up?' I said suddenly.

Humphrey, to his credit, was completely baffled by this suggestion. He didn't even seem to understand what I meant. These civil servants really are rather naïve.

'Hush it up?' he asked.

'Yes,' I said. 'Hush it up.'

'You mean,' Humphrey was apparently getting the idea at last, 'suppress it?'

I didn't exactly care for the word 'suppress', but I had to agree that that was exactly what I did mean.

Humphrey then said something like: 'I see. What you're suggesting is that, within the framework of the guidelines about Open Government which you have laid down, we should adopt a more flexible posture.' Civil servants have an extraordinary genius for wrapping up a simple idea to make it sound extremely complicated.

On second thoughts, this is a real talent which I should learn to cultivate. His phrasing might help me look as though I am not changing my posture at all.

However, we were saved by the bell as the US Cavalry galloped over the horizon in the shape of Bernard Woolley hurrying into the ante-room.

'About the Press Release,' he began breathlessly. 'There appears to have been a development which could precipitate a reappraisal of our position.'

At first I didn't quite grasp what that meant. But he then went on to say that the Department had failed to rescind the interdepartmental clearance procedure, which meant that the supplementary stop-order came into effect, which meant that it was all *all right*!

In other words, my speech didn't go out to the Press after all. By an amazing stroke of good luck, it had *only* been sent to the Prime Minister's Private Office. The Duty Office at the DDA had never received instructions to send it out *before* it was cleared with the PM and the FCO. Because of the American reference.

This wonderfully fortunate oversight seems to have saved my bacon. Of course, I didn't let Humphrey see my great sense of relief. In fact, he apologised.

'The fault is entirely mine, Minister,' he said. 'This procedure for holding up Press Releases dates back to before the era of Open Government. I unaccountably omitted to rescind it. I do hope you will forgive this lapse.'

In the circumstances, I felt that the less said the better. I decided to be magnanimous. 'That's quite all right Humphrey,' I said, 'after all, we all make mistakes.'

'Yes Minister,' said Sir Humphrey.

2
The Official
Visit

November 9th

I am finding that it is impossible to get through all the work. The diary is always full, speeches constantly have to be written and delivered, and red boxes full of papers, documents, memos, minutes, submissions and letters have to be read carefully every night. And this is only *part* of my work.

Here I am, attempting to function as a sort of managing director of a very large and important business and I have no previous experience either of the Department's work or, in fact, of management of any kind. A career in politics is no preparation for government.

And, as if becoming managing director of a huge corporation were not enough, I am also attempting to do it part-time. I constantly have to leave the DDA to attend debates in the House, to vote, to go to Cabinet and Cabinet committees and party executive meetings and I now see that it is not possible to do this job properly or even adequately. I am rather depressed.

Can anyone seriously imagine the chairman of a company leaping like a dervish out of a meeting in his office every time a bell rings, no matter when, at any time of the afternoon or evening, racing like Steve Ovett to a building eight minutes down the street, rushing through a lobby, and running back to his office to continue the meeting. This is what I have to do every time the Division Bell rings. Sometimes six or seven times in one night. And do I have any idea at all what I'm voting for? Of course I don't. How could I?

Today I arrived in the office and was immediately cast-down by the sign of my in-tray. Full to overflowing. The out-tray was completely empty.

Bernard was patiently waiting for me to read some piece of impenetrable prose that he had dug up, in answer to the question I had asked him yesterday: what are my actual powers in various far-flung parts of the UK, such as Scotland and Northern Ireland?

He proudly offered me a document. It said: 'Notwithstanding the provisions of subsection 3 of Section A of Clause 214 of the Administrative Procedures (Scotland) Act 1978, it has been agreed that, insofar as the implementation of the statutory provisions is concerned, the resolution of anomalies and uncertainties between responsible departments shall fall within the purview of the Minister for Administrative Affairs.'

I gazed blankly at it for what seemed an eternity. My mind just seemed to cloud over, as it used to at school when faced with Caesar's Gallic Wars or calculus. I longed to sleep. And it was only 9.15 a.m. I asked Bernard what it meant. He seemed puzzled by the question. He glanced at his own copy of the document.

'Well, Minister,' he began, 'it means that notwithstanding the provisions of subsection 3 of Section A of Clause 214 of . . .'

I interrupted him. 'Don't read it to me,' I said. 'I've just read it to you. What does it *mean*?'

Bernard gazed blankly at me. 'What it says, Minister.'

He wasn't trying to be unhelpful. I realised that Whitehall papers, though totally incomprehensible to people who speak ordinary English, are written in the everyday language of Whitehall Man.

Bernard hurried out into the Private Office and brought me the diary.

[*The Private Office is the office immediately adjoining the Minister's office. In it are the desks of the Private Secretary and the three or four assistant private secretaries, including the Diary Secretary – a full-time job. Adjoining the inner Private Office is the outer private office, containing about twelve people, all secretarial and clerking staff, processing replies to parliamentary questions, letters, etc.*

Access to the Minister's office is through the Private Office. Throughout the day everyone, whether outsiders or members of the Department, continually come and go through the Private Office.

The Private Office is, therefore, somewhat public – Ed.]

'May I remind you, Minister, that you are seeing a deputation from the TUC in fifteen minutes, and from the CBI half-an-hour after that, and the NEB at 12 noon.'

My feeling of despair increased. 'What do they all want – roughly?' I asked.

'They are all worried about the machinery for inflation, deflation and reflation,' Bernard informed me. What do they think I am? A

DEPARTMENT OF
ADMINISTRATIVE AFFAIRS

<u>INTERDEPARTMENTAL COMMITTE ON</u>

<u>ADMINISTRATIVE PROCEDURES</u>

<u>Minutes of a Meeting held at the Ministry of</u>

<u>Administrative Affairs on November 2nd</u>

In the Chair	Sir Humphrey Appleby KCB
Present	Mr S J Unwin CBE
	Mr H B Christie CVO
	Mrs G E Williamson OBE
	Mr P F Warburton
	Miss L W McFarlane
Secretary	Miss G Fairbairn

1. The Minutes of the previous meeting were read and agreed.

2. Matters arising:

    (i) Notwithstanding the provisions of subsection 3 of Section A of Clause 214 of the Administrative Procedures (Scotland) Act 1978, it has been agreed that, insofar as the implementation of the statutory provisions is concerned, the resolution of anomalies and uncertainties between responsible departments shall fall within the purview of the Minister for Administrative Affairs.

    /over

What does this mean? J H

30

Minister of the Crown or a bicycle pump?

I indicated the in-tray. 'When am I going to get through all this correspondence?' I asked Bernard wearily.

Bernard said: 'You *do* realise, Minister, that you don't actually *have* to?'

I had realised no such thing. This sounded good.

Bernard continued: 'If you want, we can simply draft an official reply to any letter.'

'What's an official reply?' I wanted to know.

'It just says,' Bernard explained, '"the Minister has asked me to thank you for your letter." Then *we* reply. Something like: "The matter is under consideration." Or even, if we feel so inclined, "under active consideration!"'

'What's the difference between "under consideration" and "under active consideration"?' I asked.

'"Under consideration" means we've lost the file. "Under active consideration" means we're trying to find it!'

I think this might have been one of Bernard's little jokes. But I'm not absolutely certain.

Bernard was eager to tell me what I had to do in order to lighten the load of my correspondence. 'You just transfer every letter from your in-tray to your out-tray. You put a brief note in the margin if you want to see the reply. If you don't, you need never see or hear of it again.'

I was stunned. My secretary was sitting there, seriously telling me that if I move a pile of unanswered letters from one side of my desk to the other, that is all I have to do? [*Crossman had a similar proposition offered, in his first weeks in office – Ed.*]

So I asked Bernard: 'Then what is the Minister for?'

'To make policy decisions,' he replied fluently. 'When you have decided the policy, we can carry it out.'

It seems to me that if I do not read the letters I will be somewhat ill-informed, and that therefore the number of so-called policy decisions will be reduced to a minimum.

Worse: I would not *know* which were the decisions that I needed to take. I would be dependent on my officials to tell me. I suspect that there would not be very many decisions left.

So I asked Bernard: 'How often are policy decisions needed?'

Bernard hesitated. 'Well ... from time to time, Minister,' he replied in a kindly way.

It is never too soon to get tough. I decided to start in the Department the way I meant to continue. 'Bernard,' I said firmly, *'this* government governs. It does not just preside like our predecessors did. When a nation's been going downhill you need someone to get into the driving seat, and put his foot on the accelerator.'

'I think perhaps you mean the brake, Minister,' said Bernard.

I simply do not know whether this earnest young man is being helpful, or is putting me down.

November 11th

Today I saw Sir Humphrey Appleby again. Haven't seen him for some days now.

There was a meeting in my office about the official visit to the UK of the President of Buranda. I had never even heard of Buranda.

Bernard gave me the brief last night. I found it in the third red box. But I'd had very little time to study it. I asked Humphrey to tell me about Buranda – like, where is it?

'It's fairly new, Minister. It used to be called British Equatorial Africa. It's the red bit a few inches below the Mediterranean.'

I can't see what Buranda has got to do with us. Surely this is a FCO job. [*Foreign and Commonwealth Office – Ed.*] But it was explained to me that there was an administrative problem because Her Majesty is due to be up at Balmoral when the President arrives. Therefore she will have to come to London.

This surprised me. I'd always thought that State Visits were arranged years in advance. I said so.

'This is not a State Visit,' said Sir Humphrey. 'It is a Head of Government visit.'

I asked if the President of Buranda isn't the Head of State? Sir Humphrey said that indeed he was, but also the Head of Government.

I said that, if he's merely coming as Head of Government, I didn't see why the Queen had to greet him. Humphrey said that it was because *she* is the Head of State. I couldn't see the logic. Humphrey says that the Head of State must greet a Head of State, even if the visiting Head of State is not *here* as a Head of State but only as a Head of Government.

Then Bernard decided to explain. 'It's all a matter of hats,' he said.

'Hats?' I was becoming even more confused.

'Yes,' said Bernard, 'he's coming here wearing his Head of Government hat. He is the Head of State, too, but it's not a State visit because he's not wearing his Head of State hat, but protocol demands that even though he is wearing his Head of Government hat, he must still be met by . . .' I could see his desperate attempt to avoid either mixing metaphors or abandoning his elaborately constructed simile. '. . . the Crown,' he finished in triumph.

I said that I'd never heard of Buranda anyway, and I didn't know why we were bothering with an official visit from this tin-pot little African country.

Sir Humphrey Appleby and Bernard Woolley went visibly pale. I looked at their faces, frozen in horror.

'Minister,' said Humphrey, 'I beg you not to refer to it as a tin-pot African country. It is an LDC.'

LDC is a new one on me. It seems that Buranda is what used to be called an Underdeveloped Country. However, this term has apparently become offensive, so then they were called Developing Countries. This term apparently was patronising. Then they became Less Developed Countries – or LDC, for short.

Sir Humphrey tells me that I *must* be clear on my African terminology, or else I could do irreparable damage.

It seems, in a nutshell, that the term Less Developed Countries is not yet causing offence to anyone. When it does, we are immediately ready to replace the term LDC with HRRC. This is short for Human Resource-Rich Countries. In other words, they are grossly overpopulated and begging for money. However, Buranda is *not* an HRRC. Nor is it one of the 'Haves' or 'Have-not' nations – apparently we no longer use those terms either, we talk about the North/South dialogue instead. In fact it seems that Buranda is a 'will have' nation, if there were such a term, and if it were not to cause offence to our Afro-Asian, or Third-World, or Non-Aligned-Nation brothers.

'Buranda *will have* a huge amount of oil in a couple of years from now,' confided Sir Humphrey.

'Oh I see,' I said. 'So it's not a TPLAC at all.'

Sir Humphrey was baffled. It gave me pleasure to baffle him for once. 'TPLAC?' he enquired carefully.

'Tin-Pot Little African Country,' I explained.

Sir Humphrey and Bernard jumped. They looked profoundly shocked. They glanced nervously around to check that I'd not been overheard. They were certainly not amused. How silly – anyone would think my office was bugged! [*Perhaps it was. – Ed.*]

AFRICA

MOROCCO
ALGERIA
LIBYA
EGYPT
MAURITANIA
MALI
NIGER
CHAD
SUDAN
NIGERIA
ETHIOPIA
SOMALIA
KENYA
BURANDA
ZAIRE
TANZANIA
ANGOLA
ZAMBIA
MOZAMBIQUE
NAMIBIA
BOTSWANA
SOUTH AFRICA

L.D.C.'s (Less Developed Countries)

O.E.C.'s (Over Exploitative Countries)

November 12th

On my way to work this morning I had an inspiration.

At my meeting with Humphrey yesterday it had been left for him to make arrangements to get the Queen down from Balmoral to meet the Burandan President. But this morning I remembered that we have three by-elections pending in three marginal Scottish constituencies, as a result of the death of one member who was so surprised that his constituents re-elected him in spite of his corruption and dishonesty that he had a heart attack and died, and as a result of the elevation of two other members to the Lords on the formation of the new government. [*The Peerage and/or the heart attack are, of course, the two most usual rewards for a career of corruption and dishonesty – Ed.*]

I called Humphrey to my office. 'The Queen,' I announced, 'does not have to come down from Balmoral at all.'

34

There was a slight pause.

'Are you proposing,' said Sir Humphrey in a pained manner, 'that Her Majesty and the President should exchange official greetings by telephone?'

'No.'

'Then,' said Sir Humphrey, even more pained, 'perhaps you just want them to shout very loudly.'

'Not that either,' I said cheerfully. 'We will hold the official visit in Scotland. Holyrood Palace.'

Sir Humphrey replied instantly. 'Out of the question,' he said.

'Humphrey,' I said. 'Are you sure you've given this idea due consideration?'

'It's not our decision,' he replied, 'It's an FCO matter.'

I was ready for this. I spent last night studying that wretched document which had caused me so much trouble yesterday. 'I don't think so,' I said, and produced the file with a fine flourish. 'Notwithstanding the provisions of sub-section 3 blah blah blah . . . administrative procedures blah blah blah . . . shall fall within the purview of the Minister for Administrative Affairs.' I sat back and watched.

Sir Humphrey was stumped. 'Yes, but . . . why do you want to do this?' he asked.

'It saves Her Majesty a pointless journey. And there are three marginal Scottish by-elections coming up. We'll hold them as soon as the visit is over.'

He suddenly went rather cool. 'Minister, we do not hold Head of Government visits for party political reasons, but for reasons of State.'

He had a point there. I'd slipped up a bit, but I managed to justify it okay. 'But my plan really shows that Scotland is an equal partner in the United Kingdom. She *is* Queen of Scotland too. And Scotland is full of marginal constit . . .' I stopped myself just in time, I think, '. . . depressed areas.'

But Sir Humphrey was clearly hostile to the whole brilliant notion. 'I hardly think, Minister,' he sneered, clambering onto his highest horse and looking down his patrician nose at me, 'I hardly think we can exploit our Sovereign by involving her in, if you will forgive the phrase, a squalid vote-grubbing exercise.'

I don't think there's anything squalid about grubbing for votes. I'm a democrat and proud of it and that's what democracy is all about! But I could see that I had to think up a better reason (for Civil Service consumption, at least) or else this excellent plan would be blocked somehow. So I asked Humphrey why the President of Buranda was coming to Britain.

'For an exchange of views on matters of mutual interest,' was the reply. Why does this man insist on speaking in the language of official communiqués? Or can't he help it?

'Now tell me why he's coming,' I asked with exaggerated patience. I was prepared to keep asking until I got the real answer.

'He's here to place a huge order with the British Government for offshore drilling equipment.'

Perfect! I went in for the kill. 'And where can he see all our offshore equipment? Aberdeen, Clydeside.'

Sir Humphrey tried to argue. 'Yes, but . . .'

'How many oil rigs have you got in Haslemere, Humphrey?' He wasn't pleased by this question.

'But the administrative problems . . .' he began.

I interrupted grandly: 'Administrative problems are what this whole Department was created to solve. I'm sure you can do it, Humphrey.'

'But Scotland's so remote.' He was whining and complaining now. I knew I'd got him on the run. 'Not all that remote,' I said, and pointed to the map of the UK hanging on the wall. 'It's that pink bit, about two feet above Potters Bar.'

Humphrey was not amused – 'Very droll, Minister,' he said. But *even that* did not crush me.

'It is going to be Scotland,' I said with finality. 'That is my *policy* decision. That's what I'm here for, right Bernard?'

Bernard didn't want to take sides against Humphrey, or against me. He was stuck. 'Um . . .' he said.

I dismissed Humphrey, and told him to get on with making the arrangements. He stalked out of my office. Bernard's eyes remained glued to the floor.

Bernard is *my* Private Secretary and, as such, is apparently supposed to be on my side. On the other hand, his future lies with the Department which means that he has to be on Humphrey's side. I don't see how he can possibly be on both sides. Yet, apparently, only if he succeeds in this task that is, by definition, impossible, will he continue his rapid rise to the top. It's all very puzzling. I must try and find out if I can trust him.

November 13th

Had a little chat with Bernard on our way back from Cardiff, where I addressed a conference of Municipal Treasurers and Chief Executives.

Bernard warned me that Humphrey's next move, over this Scottish business, would be to set up an interdepartmental committee to investigate and report.

I regard the interdepartmental committee as the last refuge of a desperate bureaucrat. When you can't find any argument against something you don't want, you set up an interdepartmental committee to strangle it. Slowly. I said so to Bernard.

'The same reason that politicians set up Royal Commissions,' said Bernard. This boy is no fool. I began to see why he's a high flyer.

I decided to ask Bernard what Humphrey *really* had against the idea.

'The point is,' Bernard explained, 'once they're all in Scotland the whole visit will fall within the purview of the Secretary of State for Scotland.'

I remarked that Humphrey should be pleased by this. Less work.

Bernard put me right on that immediately. Apparently the problem is that Sir Humphrey likes to go to the Palace, all dressed up in his white tie and tails and medals. But in Scotland the whole thing will be on a much smaller scale. Not so many receptions and dinners. Not so many for Sir Humphrey, anyway, only for the Perm. Sec. at the Scottish Office. Sir Humphrey might not even be invited to the return dinner as the Burandan Consulate in Edinburgh is probably exceedingly small.

I had never given the ceremonial aspect of all this any thought at all. But according to Bernard all the glitter is frightfully important to Permanent Secretaries. I asked Bernard if Humphrey had lots of medals to wear.

'Quite a few,' Bernard told me. 'Of course he got his K. a long time ago. He's a KCB. But there are rumours that he might get his G. in the next Honours list.'[1]

'How did you hear that?' I asked. I thought Honours were always a big secret.

'I heard it on the grapevine,' said Bernard.

I suppose, if Humphrey doesn't get his G., we'll hear about it on the sour-grapevine.

[*Shortly after this conversation a note was sent by Sir Humphrey to Bernard Woolley. As usual Sir Humphrey wrote in the margin – Ed.*]

[1] K. means Knighthood. KCB is Knight Commander of the Bath. G. means Grand Cross. GCB is Knight Grand Cross of the Bath.

Bernard:

Have spoken to the Perm. Sec. at the F.C.O. about official visit to Scotland.

Unfortunately, our Minister had already spoken to the Foreign Secretary. (gather they are chums.

It appears that the Cabinet is utterly united on this matter. They have blatantly issued writs for three by-elections on the day of the visit.

It seems that the Burandan Consulate is rather a hutch. V. little space at the return dinner, and I shall not be going. Rather relieved, really.

However, Perm. Sec. at F.C.O. hinted that there are rumblings in the interior. Our man in Mungoville is expecting trouble. Possibly a coup d'état.

It may be that a friendly African country with Commonwealth connections is about to become a hostile L.D.C. with a Cuban connection.

In which case, all will be well.

H.A.   13/xi

DEPARTMENT OF ADMINISTRATIVE AFFAIRS

SCHEDULE FOR THE OFFICIAL VISIT
OF THE PRESIDENT OF BURANDA

First Draft

14.00   The President disembarks, and is
        met by Her Majesty the Queen.

14.07   National Anthems:
        God Save The Queen - 0.45 secs
        Burandan Hymn - 3 minutes 25 secs
        approx.

14.11   Her Majesty the Queen and the
        President inspect Guard of Honour.

14.15   Speech of welcome by Her Majesty.

14.18   Brief reply by the President.

14.30   Proceed to cars, thence to
        Holyrood Palace.

15.00   Arrive Holyrood Palace.

[*Presumably by 'all will be well' Sir Humphrey was referring to the cancellation of the official visit, rather than another Central African country going communist – Ed.*]

November 18th

Long lapse since I made any entries in the diary. Partly due to the weekend, which was taken up with boring constituency business. And partly due to pressure of work – boring Ministerial business.

I feel that work is being kept from me. Not that I'm short of work. My boxes are full of irrelevant and unimportant rubbish.

Yesterday I really had nothing to do at all in the afternoon. No engagements of any sort. Bernard was forced to advise me to go to the House of Commons and listen to the debate there. I've never heard such a ridiculous suggestion.

Late this afternoon I was in the office, going over the plans for the Burandan visit, and I switched on the TV news. To my horror they reported a *coup d'état* in Buranda. Marxist, they think. They reported widespread international interest and concern because of Buranda's oil reserves. Not surprising. It seems that the Commander-in-Chief of the Armed Forces, who rejoices in the name of Colonel Selim Mohammed, has been declared President. Or has declared himself President, more likely. And no one knows what has happened to the former President.

I was appalled. Bernard was with me, and I told him to get me the Foreign Secretary at once.

'Shall we scramble?' he said.

'Where to?' I said, then felt rather foolish as I realised what he was talking about. Then I realised it was another of Bernard's daft suggestions: what's the point of scrambling a phone conversation about something that's just been on the television news?

I got through to Martin at the Foreign Office.

Incredibly, he knew nothing about the coup in Buranda.

'How do you know?' he asked when I told him.

'It's on TV. Didn't you know? You're the Foreign Secretary, for God's sake.'

'Yes,' said Martin, 'but my TV set's broken.'

I could hardly believe my ears. 'Your TV set? Don't you get the Foreign Office telegrams?'

Martin said: 'Yes, but they don't come in till much later. A couple of days, maybe. I always get the Foreign News from the telly.'

I thought he was joking. It seems he was not. I said that we must make sure that the official visit was still on, come what may. There are three by-elections hanging on it. He agreed.

I rang off, but not before telling Martin to let me know if he heard any more details.

Martin said: 'No, you let *me* know. You're the one with the TV set.'

November 19th

Meeting with Sir Humphrey first thing this morning. He was very jovial, beaming almost from ear to ear.

'You've heard the sad news, Minister?' he began, smiling broadly. I nodded.

'It's just a slight inconvenience,' he went on, and made a rotary gesture with both hands. 'The wheels are in motion, it's really quite simple to cancel the arrangements for the visit.'

'You'll do no such thing,' I told him.

'But Minister, we have no choice.'

'We have,' I countered. 'I've spoken to the Foreign Secretary already.' His face seemed to twitch a bit. 'We are reissuing the invitation to the new President.'

'New President?' Humphrey was aghast. 'But we haven't even recognised his government.'

I made the same rotary gesture with my hands. 'The wheels are in motion,' I smiled. I was enjoying myself at last.

Humphrey said: 'We don't know who he is.'

'Somebody Mohammed,' I explained.

'But . . . we don't know anything about him. What's he like?'

I pointed out, rather wittily I thought, that we were not considering him for membership of the Athenaeum Club. I said that I didn't give a stuff what he was like.

Sir Humphrey tried to get tough. 'Minister,' he began, 'there is total confusion in Buranda. We don't know who is behind him. We don't know if he's Soviet-backed, or just an ordinary Burandan who's gone berserk. We cannot take diplomatic risks.'

'The government has no choice,' I said.

Sir Humphrey tried a new tack. 'We have not done the paperwork.' I ignored this rubbish. Paperwork is the religion of the Civil Service. I can just imagine Sir Humphrey Appleby on his deathbed, surrounded by wills and insurance claim forms, looking up and saying, 'I cannot go yet, God, I haven't done the paperwork.'

Sir Humphrey pressed on. 'The Palace insists that Her Majesty be properly briefed. This is not possible without the paperwork.'

I stood up. 'Her Majesty will cope. She always does.' Now I had put him in the position of having to criticise Her Majesty.

He handled it well. He stood up too. 'Out of the question,' he replied. 'Who *is* he? He might not be properly brought up. He might be rude to her. He might . . . take liberties!' The mind boggles. 'And he is bound to be photographed with Her Majesty – what if he then turns out to be another Idi Amin? The repercussions are too hideous to contemplate.'

I must say the last point does slightly worry me. But not as much as throwing away three marginals. I spelt out the contrary arguments to Humphrey. 'There are reasons of State,' I said, 'which make this visit essential. Buranda is potentially enormously rich. It needs oil rigs. We have idle shipyards on the Clyde. Moreover, Buranda is strategically vital to the government's African policy.'

'The government hasn't got an African policy,' observed Sir Humphrey.

'It has now,' I snapped. 'And if the new President is Marxist-backed, who better to win him over to our side than Her Majesty? Furthermore, the people of Scotland have been promised an important State occasion and we cannot go back on our word.'

'Not to mention,' added Sir Humphrey drily, 'three by-elections in marginal constituencies.'

'That has nothing to do with it,' I said, and glowered at him. He said, 'Of course not, Minister,' but I'm not quite sure that he believed me.

Then the phone rang. Bernard took the call. It was from Martin at the FCO.

Bernard listened, then told us that the new President of Buranda had announced his intention to visit Britain next week, in line with his predecessor's arrangements.

I was impressed. The Foreign Office was getting the news at last. I asked Bernard if the cables had come through from Mungoville. 'Not exactly,' he said. 'The Foreign Secretary's driver heard a news flash on his car radio.'

The upshot is that it would now be up to the PM to cancel the visit on my recommendation or Martin's. And I have decided it is on. Another policy decision. Quite a lot of them after all. Good.

November 26th

Today was the first day of the long-awaited official visit. President Mohammed's arrival was shown on TV, Bernard and I were watching in the office – I must admit I was slightly on tenterhooks in case he did turn out to be a bit uncouth.

A jumbo jet touched down, with BURANDAN AIRWAYS written on the side. I was hugely impressed. British Airways are having to pawn their Concordes, and here is this tiny African state with its own airline, jumbo jets and all.

I asked Bernard how many planes Burandan Airways had. 'None,' he said.

I told him not to be silly and use his eyes. 'No Minister, it belongs to Freddie Laker,' he said. 'They chartered it last week and repainted it specially.' Apparently most of the Have-Nots (I mean, LDC's) do this – at the opening of the UN General Assembly the runways of Kennedy Airport are jam-packed with phoney flag-carriers. 'In fact,' added Bernard with a sly grin, 'there was one 747 that belonged to nine different African Airlines in one month. They called it the mumbo-jumbo.'

While we watched nothing much happened on the TV except the mumbo-jumbo taxiing around Prestwick and the Queen looking a bit chilly. Bernard gave me the day's schedule and explained that I was booked on the night sleeper from Euston to Edinburgh because I had to vote in a three-line whip at the House tonight and would have to miss the last plane. Then the commentator, in that special hushed BBC voice used for any occasion with which Royalty is connected, announced reverentially that we were about to catch our first glimpse of President Selim.

And out of the plane stepped Charlie. My old friend Charlie Umtali. We were at LSE together. Not Selim Mohammed at all, but Charlie.

Bernard asked me if I were sure. Silly question. How could you forget a name like Charlie Umtali?

I sent Bernard for Sir Humphrey, who was delighted to hear that we now know something about our official visitor.

Bernard's official brief said nothing. Amazing. Amazing how little the FO has been able to find out. Perhaps they were hoping it would all be on the car radio. All the brief says is that Colonel Selim Mohammed was converted to Islam some years ago, they didn't know his original name, and therefore knew little of his background.

I was able to tell Humphrey and Bernard *all* about his background. Charlie was a red-hot political economist, I informed them. Got the top first. Wiped the floor with everyone.

Bernard seemed relieved. 'Well that's all right then.'

'Why?' I enquired.

'I think Bernard means,' said Sir Humphrey helpfully, 'that he'll know how to behave if he was at an English University. Even if it was the LSE.' I never know whether or not Humphrey is insulting me intentionally.

Humphrey was concerned about Charlie's political colour. 'When you said he was red-hot, were you speaking politically?'

In a way I was. 'The thing about Charlie is that you never quite know where you are with him. He's the sort of chap who follows you into a revolving door and comes out in front.'

'No deeply held convictions?' asked Sir Humphrey.

'No. The only thing Charlie was deeply committed to was Charlie.'

'Ah, I see. A politician, Minister.'

This was definitely one of Humphrey's little jokes. He'd never be so rude otherwise. Though sometimes I suspect that Humphrey says things he really means and excuses himself by saying 'only joking'. Nonetheless, I was able to put him down by patronising him with his own inimitable phrase. 'Very droll, Humphrey,' I said cuttingly. And I pointed out that as Charlie was only here for a couple of days he couldn't do much harm anyway.

Sir Humphrey still seemed concerned. 'Just remember, Minister,' he said, 'you wanted him here, not me.'

'If you'll excuse me, Humphrey, I must get on with my letters,' I said, trying to hide my irritation.

'Just before you do,' said Sir Humphrey, 'I'd be most grateful if you would glance at this brief on African politics.' He handed me a very bulky file. More paper. I declined to read it.

'No thanks,' I said. 'I think I'm all right on all that.'

'Oh good,' he said cheerfully, 'because one wouldn't want to upset the delicate power balance between FROLINAT and FRETELIN, would one?'

I think he could see that he'd got me there. So he pressed home his advantage. 'I mean, if the new President is more sympathetic to ZIPRA than ZANLA, not to mention ZAPU and ZANU, then CARECOM and COREPER might want to bring in GRAPO, and of course that would mean going back over all that old business with ECOSOC and UNIDO and then the whole IBRD−OECD row could blow up again . . . and what would HMG do if that happened?'[1]

---

[1] FROLINAT was the National Liberation Front of Chad, a French acronym. FRETELIN was the Trust For the Liberation of Timor, a small Portuguese colony seized by Indonesia: a Portuguese acronym. ZIPRA was the Zimbabwe People's Revolutionary Army, ZANLA the Zimbabwe African Liberation Army, (cont.)

43

The only initials I understood in that whole thing were HMG [*Her Majesty's Government –Ed.*] As he had predicted, I said – as casually as I could – that I might as well glance through it.

'I'll see you on the train,' he said, and departed smoothly. I'm afraid he won a small moral victory there.

Bernard then tried to hurry me along to the House. But the huge pile of correspondence in my in-tray was now multiplying horrifyingly and apparently reproducing itself. 'What about all this,' I said helplessly. 'What can I do?'

'Well, Minister . . .' began Bernard, and his eyes flickered almost imperceptibly across to the out-tray a couple of times. I realised that I had very little choice. I picked up the whole pile of letters and moved them solemnly from the in-tray to the out-tray.

It was a funny feeling. I felt both guilty and relieved.

Bernard seemed to think I'd done the right thing. The inevitable thing, perhaps. 'That's right, Minister,' he said in a kindly tone, 'better out than in.'

November 27th

Last night was a horrendous experience, one that I do not intend to repeat in a hurry.

And today a massive crisis has yet to be solved. And it's all my fault. And I don't know if I can carry it off. Oh God!

I am sitting up in bed in a first-class sleeper, writing this diary, and dreading what the day has in store for me.

To begin at the beginning. Roy drove me from the House to Euston. I was there in plenty of time. I found my sleeper, ordered my morning tea and biscuits, the train was just pulling out of the station and my trousers were half off when there was a panic-stricken knocking on the door.

'Who is it?' I called.

(cont.) ZAPU the Zimbabwe African People's Union, ZANU the Zimbabwe African National Union. CARECOM is the acronym for the Caribbean Common Market and COREPER the Committee of Permanent Representatives to the European Community – a French acronym, pronounced co-ray-pair. ECOSOC was the Economic and Social Council of the UN, UNIDO the United Nations Industrial Development Organisation, IBRD the International Bank for Construction and Redevelopment and OECD was the Organisation for European Co-operation and Development. GRAPO could not conceivably have been relevant to the conversation, as it is the Spanish acronym for the First of October Anti-Fascist Resistance Group.

It is not impossible that Sir Humphrey may have been trying to confuse his Minister.

'Bernard,' said Bernard's voice. It was Bernard. I let him in. He was breathless and sweating. I'd never seen him in such a state. Come to think of it, I've never seen any civil servant in such a state. They all seem so frightfully calm and controlled most of the time, in a funny way it's rather reassuring to see that they sometimes panic just like the rest of the human race, and that when they do they just run around like headless chickens.

Bernard was clutching a pile of large brown manila envelopes.

'Come in Bernard,' I said soothingly. 'Whatever's the matter?'

'Read this Minister,' he said dramatically, and thrust one of the brown envelopes at my chest.

I was thoroughly irritated. Bernard is endlessly pushing paper at me. I already had four red boxes on my bunk.

I thrust the envelope back at him. 'No I won't,' I said.

'You must,' he said, and back it came as though we were playing pass the parcel. 'This is top priority.'

'You always say that about everything,' I pointed out, and carried on removing my trousers.

Bernard informed me that he was offering me an advance copy of President Selim's speech for tomorrow (today now – oh my God!) which had been sent around by the Burandan Embassy.

I wasn't interested. These speeches are always the same: happy to be here, thanks for the gracious welcome, ties between our two countries, bonds of shared experience, happy and fruitful co-operation in the future, and all the usual drivel.

Bernard agreed that all of that rubbish was in the speech, but insisted that I read the important bits at once – bits he'd underlined in red ink. He then said he was distributing copies around the train. Round the train? I thought he'd gone completely crackers – but he explained that Sir Humphrey and the Foreign Secretary and the Perm. Sec. to the Foreign Sec. and our Press officer and assorted other dignitaries were on the train. I hadn't realised.

I opened the envelope and saw the most appalling sight. A speech that we *cannot* allow to be delivered.

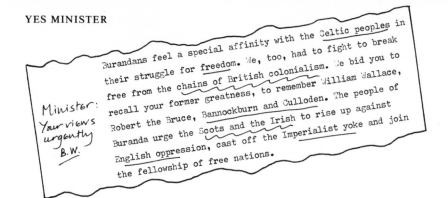

Burandans feel a special affinity with the Celtic peoples in their struggle for freedom. We, too, had to fight to break free from the chains of British colonialism. We bid you to recall your former greatness, to remember William Wallace, Robert the Bruce, Bannockburn and Culloden. The people of Buranda urge the Scots and the Irish to rise up against English oppression, cast off the Imperialist yoke and join the fellowship of free nations.

Minister:
Your views
urgently
B.W.

Then Sir Humphrey came in, wearing, incidentally, a rather startling gold silk dressing gown with a red Chinese dragon all over it. I would never have thought of Humphrey in such a garment. Perhaps I wasn't all that impressive, in my shirt-tails and socks.

'Well Minister,' Sir Humphrey began, 'we appear to have been caught with our trousers down.' He went on to say that he didn't like to say that he'd told me so, but he'd told me so.

'We're going to have egg all over our faces,' I said.

'Not egg, Minister,' he replied suavely, 'just imperialist yoke.'

I asked him if he was trying to be funny. Because I certainly can't see anything funny about this situation. I think he said, 'No, just my little yoke,' but because of the noise of the train I'm not absolutely sure.

I reiterated that something had to be done. Three Scottish by-elections hang in the balance, not counting the effects on Ulster! 'This is a catastrophe,' I whispered.

Sir Humphrey did not exactly seem to be at pains to minimise the situation. 'It is indeed,' he agreed solemnly, piling on the agony. 'A catastrophe. A tragedy. A cataclysmic, apocalyptic, monumental calamity.' He paused for breath, and then added bluntly: 'And you did it.'

This was not exactly helping. 'Humphrey,' I reproached him. 'You're paid to advise me. Advise me!'

'All in all,' replied Sir Humphrey, 'this is not unlike trying to advise the Captain of the *Titanic* after he has struck the iceberg.'

'Come on,' I said, 'there must be *something* we can do.'

'We could sing *Abide with Me*.'

There was more knocking on the door and Bernard popped in. 'Minister, the Foreign Secretary would like a word.'

Martin came in.

'Ah, Foreign Secretary.' Sir Humphrey was being obsequious now.

'Yes,' said Martin. He knew who he was. 'You've read the speech?'

Before I could reply, Sir Humphrey interrupted: 'Yes, my Minister is concerned that the government will have egg all over its face. Scotch egg, presumably.'

I'm getting a bit tired of Humphrey's stupid puns. I asked Martin why Selim Mohammed would want to make such a speech here. Martin reckons it's for home consumption, to show the other African readers that he is a pukkah anti-colonialist.

Bernard popped his head round the door, and suggested that we draft a statement in response to the speech. I thought that was a good idea. Whereupon he announced that he had brought along Bill Pritchard from the Press Office.

We had me and Humphrey and Martin and Bernard already in my sleeper. Bill Pritchard turned out to have the build of a rugger front-row forward. 'Room for a little 'un?' he enquired jovially, and knocked Humphrey forward onto the bunk, face first.

I asked Humphrey if a statement was a good idea.

'Well Minister,' he replied carefully as he stood up, still the mandarin in spite of his silly Chinese dressing gown. 'In practical terms we have, in fact, the usual six options. One, do nothing. Two, issue a statement deploring the speech. Three, lodge an official protest. Four, cut off aid. Five, break off diplomatic relations. Six, declare war.'

This sounded like rather a lot of options. I was pleased. I asked him which we should do.

'One: if we do nothing we implicitly agree with the speech. Two: if we issue a statement we just look foolish. Three: if we lodge a protest it will be ignored. Four: we can't cut off aid because we don't give them any. Five: if we break off diplomatic relations we cannot negotiate the oil rig contracts. Six: if we declare war it just *might* look as if we were over-reacting.' He paused. 'Of course, in the old days we'd have sent in a gunboat.'

I was desperate by this time. I said, 'I suppose that is absolutely out of the question?'

They all gazed at me in horror. Clearly it is out of the question.

Bernard had absented himself during Humphrey's résumé of the possibilities. Now he squeezed back into the compartment.

'The Permanent Under-Secretary to the Foreign and Commonwealth Office is coming down the corridor,' he announced.

'Oh terrific,' muttered Bill Pritchard. 'It'll be like the Black Hole of

47

Calcutta in here.'

Then I saw what he meant. Sir Frederick Stewart, Perm. Sec. of the FCO, known as 'Jumbo' to his friends, burst open the door. It smashed Bernard up against the wall. Martin went flying up against the washbasin, and Humphrey fell flat on his face on the bunk. The mighty mountain of lard spoke:

'May I come in, Minister?' He had a surprisingly small high voice.

'You can try,' I said.

'This is all we needed,' groaned Bill Pritchard as the quivering mass of flesh forced its way into the tiny room, pressing Bill up against the mirror and me against the window. We were all standing extremely close together.

'Welcome to the Standing Committee,' said Humphrey as he propped himself precariously upright.

'What do we do about this hideous thing? This hideous *speech*, I mean,' I added nervously, in case Jumbo took offence. His bald head shone, reflecting the overhead lamp.

'Well now,' began Jumbo, 'I think we know what's behind this, don't we Humpy?'

Humpy? Is this his nickname? I looked at him with new eyes. He clearly thought I was awaiting a response.

'I think that Sir Frederick is suggesting that the offending paragraph of the speech may be, shall we say, a bargaining counter.'

'A move in the game,' said Jumbo.

'The first shot in a battle,' said Humphrey.

'An opening gambit,' said Bernard.

These civil servants are truly masters of the cliché. They can go on all night. They do, unless stopped. I stopped them.

'You mean, he wants something,' I said incisively. It's lucky someone was on the ball.

'If he doesn't,' enquired Jumbo Stewart, 'why give us a copy in advance?' This seems unarguable. 'But unfortunately the usual channels are blocked because the Embassy staff are all new and we've only just seen the speech. And no one knows anything about this new President.'

I could see Humphrey giving me meaningful looks.

'I do,' I volunteered, slightly reluctantly.

Martin looked amazed. So did Jumbo.

'They were at University together.' Humphrey turned to me. 'The old boy network?' It seemed to be a question.

I wasn't awfully keen on this turn of events. After all, it's twenty-five years since I saw Charlie, he might not remember me, I don't know what I can achieve. 'I think you ought to see him, Sir Frederick,' I replied.

'Minister, I think you carry more weight,' said Jumbo. He seemed unaware of the irony.

There was a pause, during which Bill Pritchard tried unsuccessfully to disguise a snigger by turning it into a cough.

'So we're all agreed,' enquired Sir Humphrey, 'that the mountain should go to Mohammed?'

'No, *Jim's* going,' said Martin, and got a very nasty look from his overweight Perm. Sec. and more sounds of a Press officer asphyxiating himself.

I realised that I had no choice. 'All right,' I agreed, and turned to Sir Humphrey, 'but you're coming with me.'

'Of course, said Sir Humphrey, 'I'd hardly let you do it on your own.'

Is this *another* insult, or is it just my paranoia?

Later today:
Charlie Umtali – perhaps I'd better call him President Selim from now on – welcomed us to his suite at the Caledonian Hotel at 10.00 a.m.

'Ah Jim.' He rose to greet us courteously. I had forgotten what beautiful English he spoke. 'Come in, how nice to see you.'

I was actually rather, well, gratified by this warm reception.

'Charlie,' I said. We shook hands. 'Long time no see.'

'You don't have to speak pidgin English to me,' he said, turned to his aide, and asked for coffee for us all.

I introduced Humphrey, and we all sat down.

'I've always thought that Permanent Under-Secretary is such a demeaning title,' he said. Humphrey's eyebrows shot up.

'I beg your pardon?'

'It sounds like an assistant typist or something,' said Charlie pleasantly, and Humphrey's eyebrows disappeared into his hairline. 'Whereas,' he continued in the same tone, 'you're really in charge of everything, aren't you?' Charlie hasn't changed a bit.

Humphrey regained his composure and preened. 'Not quite everything.'

I then congratulated Charlie on becoming Head of State. 'Thank you,' he said, 'though it wasn't difficult. I didn't have to do any of the boring things like fighting elections.' He paused, and then added casually 'Or by-elections,' and smiled amiably at us.

Was this a hint? I decided to say nothing. So after a moment he went on. 'Jim, of course I'm delighted to see you, but is this purely a social visit or is there anything you particularly wanted to talk about? Because I do have to put the finishing touches to my speech.'

Another hint?

I told him we'd seen the advance copy. He asked if we liked it. I asked him if, as we were old friends, I could speak frankly. He nodded.

I tried to make him realise that the bit about colonialist oppression was slightly – well, really, *profoundly* embarrassing. I asked him if he couldn't just snip out the whole chunk about the Scots and the Irish.

Charlie responded by saying, 'This is something that I feel very deeply to be true. Surely the British don't believe in suppressing the truth?'

A neat move.

Sir Humphrey then tried to help. 'I wonder if there is anything that might persuade the President to consider recasting the sentence in question so as to transfer the emphasis from the specific instance to the abstract concept, without impairing the conceptual integrity of the theme?'

Some help.

I sipped my coffee with a thoughtful expression on my face.

Even Charlie hadn't got it, I don't think, because he said, after quite a pause: 'While you're here Jim, may I sound you out on a proposal I was going to make to the Prime Minister at our talks?'

I nodded.

He then told us that his little change of government in Buranda had alarmed some of the investors in their oil industry. Quite unnecessarily, in his view. So he wants some investment from Britain to tide him over.

At last we were talking turkey.

I asked how much. He said fifty million pounds.

Sir Humphrey looked concerned. He wrote me a little note. 'Ask him on what terms.' So I asked.

'Repayment of the capital not to start before ten years. And interest free.'

It sounded okay to me, but Humphrey choked into his coffee. So I pointed out that fifty million was a lot of money.

'Oh well, in that case . . .' began Charlie, and I could see that he was about to end the meeting.

'But let's talk about it,' I calmed him down. I got another note from Humphrey, which pointed out that, if interest ran at ten per cent on average, and if the loan was interest free for ten years, he was in effect asking for a free gift of fifty million pounds.

Cautiously, I put this point to Charlie. He very reasonably (I thought) explained that it was all to our advantage, because they would use the loan to buy oil rigs built on the Clyde.

I could see the truth of this, but I got another frantic and, by now, almost illegible note from Humphrey, saying that Charlie wants us to give him fifty million pounds so that he can buy our oil rigs with our money. (His underlinings, I may say.)

We couldn't go on passing notes to each other like naughty school-boys, so we progressed to muttering. 'It sounds pretty reasonable to me,' I whispered.

'You can't be serious,' Humphrey hissed.

'Lots of jobs,' I countered, and I asked Charlie, if we did such a deal, would he make appropriate cuts in his speech? This was now cards on the table.

Charlie feigned surprise at my making this connection, but agreed that he would make cuts. However, he'd have to know right away.

'Blackmail,' Sir Humphrey had progressed to a stage whisper that could be heard right across Princes Street.

'Are you referring to me or to my proposal?' asked Charlie.

'Your proposal, naturally,' I said hastily and then realised this was a trick question. 'No, not even your proposal.'

I turned to Humphrey, and said that I thought we could agree to this. After all, there are precedents for this type of deal.[1]

Sir Humphrey demanded a private word with me, so we went and stood in the corridor.

I couldn't see why Humphrey was so steamed up. Charlie had offered us a way out.

Humphrey said we'd never get the money back, and therefore he could not recommend it to the Treasury and the Treasury would

[1] Hacker might perhaps have been thinking of the Polish shipbuilding deal during the Callaghan government, by which the UK lent money interest free to the Poles, so that they could buy oil tankers from us with our money, tankers which were then going to compete against our own shipping industry. These tankers were to be built on Tyneside, a Labour-held marginal with high unemployment. It could have been said that the Labour government was using public money to buy Labour votes, but no one did – perhaps because, like germ warfare, no one wants to risk using an uncontrollable weapon that may in due course be used against oneself.

never recommend it to Cabinet. 'You are proposing,' he declared pompously, 'to buy your way out of a political entanglement with fifty million pounds of public money.'

I explained that this is diplomacy. He said it was corruption. I said 'GCB,' only just audibly.

There was a long pause.

'What did you say, Minister?'

'Nothing,' I said.

Humphrey suddenly looked extremely thoughtful. 'On the other hand...' he said, '...we don't want the Soviets to invest in Buranda, do we?' I shook my head. 'Yes, I see what you mean,' he murmured.

'And they will if we don't,' I said, helping him along a bit.

Humphrey started to marshal all the arguments on my side. 'I suppose we could argue that we, as a part of the North/South dialogue, have a responsibility to the ...'

'TPLAC's?' I said.

Humphrey ignored the crack. 'Quite,' he said. 'And if we were to insist on one per cent of the equity in the oil revenues ten years from now ... yes, on balance, I think we can draft a persuasive case in terms of our third-world obligations, to bring in the FCO ... and depressed area employment, that should carry with us both the Department of Employment and the Scottish Office ... then the oil rig construction should mobilise the Department of Trade and Industry, and if we can reassure the Treasury that the balance of payments wouldn't suffer ... Yes, I think we might be able to mobilise a consensus on this.'

I thought he'd come to that conclusion. We trooped back into Charlie's room.

'Mr President,' said Sir Humphrey, 'I think we can come to terms with each other after all.'

'You know my price,' said Charlie.

'And you know mine,' I said. I smiled at Sir Humphrey. 'Everyone has his price, haven't they?'

Sir Humphrey looked inscrutable again. Perhaps this is why they are called mandarins.

'Yes Minister,' he replied.

3
The Economy Drive

December 1

On the train going up to town after a most unrestful weekend in the constituency, I opened up the *Daily Mail*. There was a huge article making a personal attack on me.

I looked around the train. Normally the first-class compartment is full of people reading *The Times*, *The Telegraph*, or the *FT*. Today they all seemed to be reading the *Daily Mail*.

Let's get rid of Jim Hacker

By JOHN PILGRIM
Special Investigator

THE RIGHT HONOURABLE Jim Hacker, MP promised to carry out the government's pledge to slim down the Civil Service, to wipe out the interference from Whitehall and Town Hall busybodies. But how many people realise that the Civil Service is, growing, like Topsy, every day?

I have discovered that no less than *four* Ministries check the supply of the same army uniforms. The Ministry of Defence checks to see that they have

ordered. The Department of Trade and Industry checks to see that they have been manufactured according to government regulations. The Department of Employment checks that the Manufacturer falls in with the Manpower Planning Standards, and Jim Hacker's mob just checks up on everybody else!

Jim Hacker is the most obvious case of overmanning in Whitehall. Let's start by getting rid of him and saving at least one salary.

When I got to the office Bernard offered me the paper and asked me if I'd read it. I told him I'd read it. Bernard told me that Frank had read it, and wanted to see me. Then Frank came in and asked me if I'd read it. I told him I'd read it.

Frank then read it to me. I don't know why he read it to me. I told him I'd read it. It seemed to make him feel better to read it aloud. It made me feel worse.

I wondered how many copies they sell every day. 'Two million, three million?' I asked Bernard.

'Oh *no*, Minister,' he answered as if my suggested figures were an utterly outrageous overestimate.

I pressed him for an answer. 'Well, how many?'

'Um . . . four million,' he said with some reluctance. 'So only . . . twelve million people have read it. Twelve or fifteen. And lots of their readers can't read, you know.'

Frank was meanwhile being thoroughly irritating. He kept saying, 'have you read this?' and reading another appalling bit out of it. For instance: 'Do *you* realise that more people serve in the Inland Revenue than the Royal Navy?' This came as news to me, but Bernard nodded to confirm the truth of it when I looked at him.

' "Perhaps," ' said Frank, *still* reading aloud from that bloody paper, ' "Perhaps the government thinks that a tax is the best form of defence" '.

Bernard sniggered, till he saw that I was not amused. He tried to change his snigger into a cough. The man's a fool.

Frank then informed me, as if I didn't already know, that this article is politically very damaging, and that I had to make slimming down the Civil Service a priority. There's no doubt that he's right, but it's just not that easy.

I pointed this out to Frank. 'You know what?' he said angrily. 'You're house-trained already.'

I didn't deign to reply. Besides, I couldn't think of an answer.

[*The Civil Service phrase for making a new Minister see things their way is 'house-training'. When a Minister is so house-trained that he automatically sees everything from the Civil Service point-of-view, this is known in Westminster as the Minister having 'gone native' – Ed.*]

Sir Humphrey came in, brandishing a copy of the *Daily Mail*. 'Have you read this?' he began.

This was too much. I exploded. 'Yes. Yes! Yes!!! I have read that sodding newspaper. *I* have read it, *you* have read it, *we have all bloody read it*. DO I MAKE MYSELF CLEAR?'

'Abundantly, Minister,' said Sir Humphrey coldly, after a brief pained silence.

I recovered my temper, and invited them all to sit down. 'Humphrey,' I said, 'we simply *have* to slim down the Civil Service. How many people are there in this department?'

'This department?' He seemed evasive. 'Oh well, we're very small.'

'How small?' I asked, and receiving no reply, I decided to hazard a guess. 'Two thousand? . . . three thousand?' I suggested, fearing the worst.

'About twenty-three thousand I think, Minister?'

I was staggered. Twenty-three thousand people? In the Department of Administrative Affairs? Twenty-three thousand administrators, all to administer other administrators?

'We'll have to do an O & M,' I said. [*Organisation and Method Study – Ed.*] 'See how many we can do without.'

'We did one of those last year,' said Sir Humphrey blandly. 'And we discovered we needed another five hundred people. However, Minister, we could always close your Bureaucratic Watchdog Department.'[1]

I'd been expecting this. I know Humphrey doesn't like it. How could he? But we are not cutting it. Firstly, it's a very popular measure with the voters. And secondly, it's the only thing I've achieved since I've been here. 'It is a chance for the ordinary citizen to help us find ways to stop wasting government money,' I reiterated.

'The public,' said Sir Humphrey, 'do not know anything about wasting public money. We are the experts.'

I grinned. 'Can I have that in writing?'

Humphrey got very tetchy. 'You know that's not what I meant,' he snapped. 'The Watchdog Office is merely a troublemaker's letter box.'

'It stays,' I replied.

We gazed at each other, icily. Finally Sir Humphrey said: 'Well, offhand, I don't know what other economies to suggest.'

This was ludicrous. 'Are you seriously trying to tell me,' I asked, 'that there's nothing we can cut down on?'

He shrugged. 'Well . . . I suppose we could lose one or two of the tea ladies.'

I exploded again. I told him not to be ridiculous. I told him I wanted facts, answers. I listed them:

[1]The Bureaucratic watchdog was an innovation of Hacker's, to which members of the public were invited to report any instances of excessive government bureaucracy which they encountered personally. It was disbanded after four months.

1 How many people work here?
2 What do they all do?
3 How many buildings do we have?
4 Who and what is in these buildings?

I spelt it out. I demanded a complete study. First of all we'll put our own house in order. Then we'll deal with the rest of Whitehall. With a complete study, we'll be able to see where to cut costs, cut staff, and cut procedures.

Sir Humphrey listened with some impatience. 'The Civil Service, Minister,' he responded when I paused for breath, 'merely exists to implement legislation that is enacted by Parliament. So long as Parliament continues to legislate for more and more control over people's lives, the Civil Service must grow.'

'Ha!' Frank made a derisive noise.

Sir Humphrey turned towards him with a glassy stare. 'Am I to infer that Mr Weisel disagrees with me?'

'Ha!' repeated Frank.

Frank was getting on *my* nerves too. 'Frank, either laugh thoroughly, or not at all,' I instructed.

'Minister,' Humphrey stood up. 'I am fully seized of your requirements, so if you'll excuse me I think I'd better set the wheels in motion.'

After Sir H. left Frank told me that there was a cover-up going on. Apparently a North West Regional controller has achieved cuts of £32 million in his region alone. And the Civil Service has suppressed news of it. I asked why.

'They don't want cuts,' said Frank impatiently. 'Asking Sir Humphrey to slim down the Civil Service is like asking an alcoholic to blow up a distillery.'

I asked Bernard if this story were true. Bernard said that he didn't know, but, if so, he would be aghast. I asked them both to check up on it. Bernard said he'd find out through the grapevine, and I arranged with Frank to do some more ferreting.

[*Sometime in the next few days Bernard Woolley had an interview with Sir Humphrey Appleby. Sir Humphrey wrote a memo following the meeting, which we found in the DAA Personnel Files at Walthamstow – Ed.*]

Woolley came at 5.15 p.m. to discuss the £32 million saved by the NW Controller. I remarked that I was aghast.

Woolley said he also was aghast, and that it was incredible that we knew nothing of this.

He sometimes reveals himself as worryingly naïf. I, of course, know all about it. I am merely aghast that it has got out. It might result in our getting less money from the Treasury in next year's PESC review. [*PESC is the Public Expenditure Scrutiny Committee – Ed.*]

I felt I would learn more about Bernard Woolley if I made the conversation informal. [*To do so, Sir Humphrey would have moved from behind his desk to the conversation area, remarking that it was after 5.30 p.m. and offering Woolley a sherry – Ed.*] Then I asked him why he was looking worried. He revealed that he genuinely wanted the DAA to save money.

This was shocking. Clearly he has not yet grasped the fundamentals of our work.

There has to be some way to measure success in the Service. British Leyland can measure success by the size of its profits. [*British Leyland was the name of the car manufacturer into which billions of pounds of taxpayers' money was paid in the 1980s in an attempt to produce full employment in the West Midlands. To be more accurate, BL measured its failure by the size of its losses – Ed.*] However, the Civil Service does not make profits or losses. *Ergo*, we measure success by the size of our staff and our budget. By definition a big department is more successful than a small one. It seems extraordinary that Woolley could have passed through the Civil Service College without having understood that this simple proposition is the basis of our whole system.

Nobody had asked the NW controller to save £32 million. Suppose everybody did it? Suppose everybody started saving money irresponsibly all over the place?

Woolley then revealed another curious blind-spot when he advanced the argument that the Minister wanted cuts. I was obliged to explain the facts of life:

1   Ministers come, and Ministers go. The average Minister lasts less than eleven months in any Department.
    [*In his ten years as Chairman of British Steel, Sir Monty Finniston dealt with no less than nineteen Ministers at the Department of Industry. – Ed.*]

2   It is our duty to assist the Minister to fight for the Department's money despite his own panic reactions.

3   However, the Minister must be allowed to panic. Politicians like to panic. They need activity – it is their substitute for achievement.

4   The argument that we must do everything a Minister demands because he has been 'democratically chosen' does not stand up to close inspection. MP's are not chosen by 'the people' – they are chosen by their local constituency party, *i.e.* thirty-five men in grubby raincoats or thirty-five women in silly hats. The further 'selection' process is equally a nonsense: there are only 630 MP's and a party with just over 300 MP's forms a government – and of these 300, 100 are too old and too silly to be ministers, and 100 too young and too callow. Therefore there are

about 100 MP's to fill 100 government posts. Effectively no choice at all.

5 It follows that as Ministers have had no proper selection or training, it is our patriotic duty to arrange for them to make the right decision as often as possible.

I concluded by teaching Woolley how to explain the saving of £32 million to the Minister. I offered the following possibilities. Say that:

    (a) they have changed their accounting system in the North-West.

or (b) redrawn the boundaries, so that this year's figures are not comparable.

or (c) the money was compensation for special extra expenditure of £16 million a year over the last two years, which has now stopped.

or (d) it is only a paper saving, so it will all have to be spent next year.

or (e) a major expenditure is late in completion, and therefore the region will be correspondingly over budget next year. [*Known technically as phasing – Ed.*]

or (f) there has been an unforeseen but important shift of personnel and industries to other regions whose expenditure rose accordingly.

or (g) some large projects were cancelled for reasons of economy early in the accounting period with the result that the expenditure was not incurred but the budget had already been allocated.

Woolley seemed to understand. I am concerned that he has not had adequate training so far. I intend to keep a close watch on him because, in spite of all this, I still think he shows promise.

He volunteered information that Frank Weisel was ferreting. Naturally, I arranged a government car to assist him. [*It was standard Civil Service practice to provide government cars for troublesome outsiders. The driver would be relied on to, at the very least, report where he had been, if only to account for the mileage.*

Drivers are one of the most useful sources of information in Whitehall. Their passengers are frequently indiscreet, forgetting that everything they say in the back seat can be overheard in the front. Furthermore, Ministers tend to forget confidential documents, and leave them behind in the car.

Information is Whitehall's most valuable currency. Drivers barter information. – Ed.]

[*The following series of memos between Sir Humphrey Appleby and Sir Frederick Stewart were found in a Ministry file. – Ed.*]

A note from Sir Frederick Stewart, Permanent Secretary to the FCO:

Foreign and Commonwealth Office
From the Permanent Under Secretary of State

Dear Humpy,   12/xii

    Am concerned that
your minister is still trying
to economise pointlessly.

        Jumbo

A reply from Sir Humphrey to Sir Frederick Stewart:

DEPARTMENT OF
ADMINISTRATIVE AFFAIRS

From the Permanent Under–Secretary of State

Dear Jumbo —

Am hoping it will be like all the
other government economy drives —
three days of press releases, three weeks
of ministerial memos, then a crisis in
the Middle East, and back to normal
again.

H.

12 . xii

A reply from Sir Frederick:

Foreign and Commonwealth Office
From the Permanent Under Secretary of State

13/vii

Dear Humpy,

Hope you're right, but why take chances? I suggest another 'Operation Hairshirt'

"Economy begins at home. Set a personal example. Can't expect others to do what we don't do ourselves." etc.

Jumbo,

A reply from Sir Humphrey:

**DEPARTMENT OF
ADMINISTRATIVE AFFAIRS**

From the Permanent Under–Secretary of State

Jumbo —

Good idea . Will try it . Thanks.
Self - denial is probably the answer,
as always.

J.

P.S. See you at the Lord Mayor's
dinner .

13 xii

[Hackers's diary continues – Ed.]
December 15th

Today we had the big meeting on expenditure cuts. Frank has been ferreting for a couple of weeks. The meeting didn't actually end the way I thought it would, but we do now have a real programme of action, though not the one I expected.

At the meeting were Sir Humphrey, Bernard, and Frank who had come up with what seemed to be some astounding revelations about wastage in our midst. I told Sir Humphrey that he would be pretty surprised by it all, and that the new facts seemed to be a frightening indictment of bureaucratic sloppiness and self-indulgence.

Sir Humphrey seemed very concerned and intrigued, and was eager to learn where there might be scope for dramatic economies.

Frank had prepared two files, one on Manpower and one on Buildings. I decided to look at Buildings first.

'Chadwick House,' I began. 'West Audley Street.'

'A huge building,' said Frank, 'with only a handful of people working there.'

Sir Humphrey said he happened to know about Chadwick House. 'It is certainly under-used at the moment, but it is the designated office for the new Commission on the Environment. We're actually wondering if it'll be big enough when all the staff move in.'

This seemed fair enough. So I went on to Ladysmith Buildings, Walthamstow. It is totally empty.

'Of course,' said Sir Humphrey.

I asked him what he meant.

'Security, Minister, I can say no more.'

'Do you mean MI6?' I asked.

Sir Humphrey shook his head, and said nothing. So I asked him what he *did* mean.

'We do not admit that MI6 exists,' he replied.

I've never heard anything so daft. I pointed out that absolutely everyone knows that it exists.

'Nevertheless, we do not admit it. Not everyone around this table has been vetted.'

Vetted is such a silly expression. I remarked that it sounds like something you do to cats.

'Yes, but not ferrets, Minister,' said Sir Humphrey sharply, eyeing Frank. 'Ladysmith Buildings is top secret.'

'How,' I asked sarcastically, 'can a seven-storey building in Walthamstow be a secret?'

'Where there's a will there's a way,' replied Humphrey, with (I think) a twinkle in his eye. It was all quite amicable, but I could see that he had no intention of discussing anything that was remotely to do with security while Frank was present. I had no intention of asking Frank to leave, so, reluctantly, I was forced to move on to the next two white elephants.

'Wellington House, Hyde Park Road. Estimated value, seven and a half million pounds. Westminster Old Hall, Sackville Square, estimated value, eleven million pounds. Both buildings with a tiny staff, and entirely full of filing cabinets.'

'May I ask the source of these valuations?' Sir Humphrey enquired.

'Going rate for office property in the area,' said Frank.

'Ah. *Unfortunately*,' said Sir Humphrey in his most helpful tone, 'neither building would actually fetch the going rate.'

I asked why not.

'Wellington House has no fire escape or fire doors and the fabric of the building would not stand the alteration, so it can't be sold as offices.'

'Then how can we use it?' enquired Frank aggressively.

'Government buildings do not need fire safety clearance.'

'Why?' demanded Frank.

'Perhaps,' Humphrey offered, 'because Her Majesty's Civil Servants are not easily inflamed.' This time he chuckled. Another of his little jokes. He seemed to be increasingly pleased with himself. I don't care for this.

[*In fact, government buildings have to comply with most statutory fire requirements, but not with regard to means of escape! – Ed.*]

We were not getting very far with our economies, so I asked why Westminster Old Hall couldn't be sold as offices.

'It's a Class One listed building. Can't change current user designation. The Environment, you know.'

We were getting nowhere fast. Frank moved on, and suggested we sold 3 to 17 Beaconsfield Street.

'That,' said Sir Humphrey, 'has a three level reinforced concrete basement.'

'So?' I said.

'It is there in case,' said Sir Humphrey. I waited for him to complete his sentence, but after a while it became apparent that he thought he had already done so.

'In case?' I asked eventually.

'You know, Minister,' he said, his voice pregnant with hidden meaning. 'Emergency Government Headquarters, if and when.'

I was baffled. 'If and when what?

Humphrey was now at his most enigmatic. 'If and when . . . you know what,' he replied so quietly that I could hardly hear him.

'What?' I wasn't sure I'd heard correctly.

'If and when you know what?'

'I *don't* know what,' I said confused. 'What?'

'What?' Now Sir Humphrey seemed confused.

'What do you mean, if and when you know what? If and when, I know what – *what*?'

At last Humphrey decided to make his meaning clear. 'When the chips are down, Minister, and the balloon goes up and the lights go out . . . there has to be somewhere to carry on government, even if everything else stops.'

I considered this carefully for a few moments. 'Why?' I asked.

Humphrey appeared to be absolutely staggered by this question. He explained to me, as if I were a backward five-year-old, 'Government doesn't stop merely because the country's been destroyed. Annihilation is bad enough, without anarchy to make it even worse.'

Obviously Humphrey was concerned about the danger of a lot of rebellious cinders.

However, this is clearly an MOD matter [*Ministry of Defence – Ed.*] and I can see it is beyond *my* power to do anything about 3 to 17 Beaconsfield Street.

There was one more virtually unused building on Frank's list. It was my last shot. 'What about the Central Registry?' I enquired, without any real hope.

'No planning permission,' said Sir Humphrey, with a bland smile of a man who knows he's won five rounds and is way ahead on points.

Frank suddenly intervened. 'How does he know all this?' he enquired belligerently, and turned accusingly to Sir Humphrey. 'You *knew* where I'd been.'

This hadn't occurred to me, but Frank was obviously right. I was about to lay into Humphrey on that score, when Humphrey said to me, most disarmingly: 'Of course we knew where he'd been. Why, was he supposed to be spying?'

I wasn't ready for that particular googly. I realised at once that I was on a very sticky wicket.

Humphrey pressed home his advantage. 'I mean, we *do* believe in open enquiries, don't we?'

There was no answer to this, so, in my most businesslike fashion, I closed the Buildings file. [*In any case, it would have been impossible to sell all these government buildings simultaneously. If you put government property in London on the market all at once, you would destroy the market – like diamonds. – Ed.*]

I turned to Manpower. Here, I felt I was on rock solid ground.

'Apparently,' I began, 'there are ninety civil servants in Sunderland exactly duplicating the work of ninety others here in Whitehall.'

Humphrey nodded. 'That stems from a cabinet decision. Job Creation in the North East.'

At last we were in agreement about something. 'Let's get rid of them,' I proposed.

Frank chimed in eagerly, 'Yes, that would get rid of ninety civil servants at a stroke.' Somehow, the way Frank spits out the words 'civil servants' makes them sound more contemptible than petty thieves. If I were a civil servant I think Frank's style would offend me, though Sir Humphrey doesn't seem too bothered, I must say.

But he picked up Frank's phrase 'at a stroke'. [*Actually, Edward Heath's phrase, originally applied to price reductions which – needless to say – never occurred. – Ed.*] 'Or indeed,' said Sir Humphrey, 'at a strike.'

'What?' I said.

'Personally, Minister, I should be wholeheartedly in favour of such a move. A considerable economy. But . . . I should remind you that it is a depressed area. Hence the original job creation scheme. It would show great political courage for the government to sack staff in a depressed marginal constituency.'

We sat for a while in silence. I must say, I think it was rather sporting of Humphrey to remind me that a marginal constituency was at stake. Normally civil servants take no interest in those vital political calculations.

Clearly, I couldn't possibly risk a strike up there. But I was feeling really hopeless about these economies by now. I decided to put the ball back into Humphrey's court.

'Look, Humphrey,' I said, 'this is all very well . . . but . . . well, I just don't believe that there are no savings to be made in the Civil Service. I see waste everywhere.'

'I agree with you, Minister,' came the reply, much to my surprise. 'There is indeed scope for economy . . .'

'Then . . .' I interrupted, '. . . *where*, for God's sake?'

And to my surprise, Sir Humphrey suddenly became very positive. 'I sometimes feel that the whole way we do things is on too lavish a scale. You know, cars, furnishings, private office staff, entertainment, duplicating machines. . . .'

This was marvellous. I couldn't agree more. I nodded enthusiastically.

'There is a difficulty, however,' he added. My heart sank again, but I waited to hear what it was. 'It does cause profound resentment if those at the top continue to enjoy the convenience and comforts they have withdrawn from those below them, not to mention the deeply damaging publicity. . . .'

He broke off, and waited to see how I reacted. I wasn't awfully keen, I must admit. It became clear that Humphrey's scheme was that he and I should set a personal example. Economy begins at home, and we can't expect others to do what we don't do ourselves, and so forth.

I challenged Humphrey. 'Would it really save that much?'

'Directly, no,' he said. 'But as an example to the whole public service . . . incalculable!'

Then Frank came up with the decisive argument in favour of Humphrey's plan. He pointed out that there would be lots of great publicity in it. He suggested the sort of newspaper headlines we'd be getting: THE MINISTER SHOWS THE WAY, or SLIMLINE GOVERN-MENT, HACKER SETS EXAMPLE. We might even get a first-name headline: SAVE IT, SAYS JIM.

I gave Humphrey the okay to put the scheme into practice as soon as possible. I shall be interested to see how it works. At this moment, I have high hopes.

December 19th
Sunday morning. I'm writing this at home, in the constituency.

Haven't had time to make any entries in the diary for some days because this economy drive is creating a lot of extra work for me. However, I'm sure it's all going to be worth it.

It was a dreadful journey home on Friday night. I got home in the middle of the night. Annie had gone to bed. Apparently she'd made supper for us, and it had spoiled.

I'd tried to get a taxi to get me from Whitehall to Euston, but there was a thunderstorm and no taxis were available. So I'd gone by tube, carrying three red boxes which are immensely heavy when filled, and I'd missed the train at Euston. So I got home very tired and wet.

I apologised for waking Annie, and told her about my troublesome journey.

'What happened to the chauffeur-driven car?' she asked anxiously.

'I've got rid of it,' I explained proudly. 'I've also got rid of the chauffeur, all the grand office furniture, and the drinks cabinet, and half my private office staff.'

'You've been sacked!' she said. Annie often jumps to the most ridiculous alarmist conclusions. I explained that it was an economy drive and that I was setting an example of no frills, no luxuries and no privileges.

Annie couldn't seem to understand. 'You're bloody mad!' she exploded. 'For twenty years as a backbencher you have complained that you had no facilities and no help. Now you've been given them, and you're throwing them away.'

I tried to explain it, but she wouldn't let me get a word in edgeways. 'For twenty years you've wanted to be a success – why did you want it if it brings no greater comfort than failure?'

I explained that this move would give me much greater power in the end.

Annie was unimpressed. 'And how will you travel when you're Prime Minister? Hitch-hike?'

Annie just doesn't understand the finer points of politics, I'm afraid.

December 20th

Great progress today with the economy drive.

The office work is getting a bit behind, with twelve fewer people in my Private Office. Bernard is working overtime, and so am I, but clearly we didn't need all those people out there, reading my letters and writing my letters, and making appointments and answering phones, and drafting replies to questions and – basically – protecting me from the outside world. I don't need all those people to shield me. I am the people's representative, I should be available to one and all.

However, we have to avoid screw-ups like this morning, when I arrived an hour and a half late to open a conference. What made it even more unfortunate was that it was the Business Efficiency Conference!

And, because we've abolished the night shift for cleaners (a really useful economy, in my view), I had a cleaning lady in my office vacuuming. Bernard and I had to shout at the tops of our voices as we discussed the week's diary. But I'm sure these little wrinkles can be ironed out.

Tomorrow I have a vital meeting with Mr Brough, Director of Manpower Planning for the North East Region, on the subject of staff reductions. I've never met him, but Bernard tells me he's eager to make cuts.

The biggest progress is in the media coverage I'm getting. A front page story in the *Express*. Couldn't be better.

No luxury lunches in Hacker's new austerity regime

"ECONOMY begins at home", said Jim Hacker today, as he ate a sandwich off a paper plate to set an example to Britain's pampered army of bowler-hatted bureaucrats.

SIR BERNARD WOOLLEY RECALLS:[1]

I remember Jim Hacker's first economy drive only too well. I suspected, green though I still was, that Sir Humphrey Appleby had created a potentially disastrous situation.

It was impossible for me to run the Private Office singlehanded, with just a couple of typists to help. Errors were bound to occur, and sooner or later there would be a calamity.

The calamity occurred sooner than even I expected. On 21 December, the day after Hacker had received some favourable publicity, Ron Watson arrived at the Department without an appointment. Watson was the General Secretary of the Civil Service Transport and Associated Government Workers.

He demanded to see the Minister at once, because of what he described as 'disturbing' rumours about cut-backs and redundancies affecting his members. The rumours were clearly generated by the numerous Press stories of which Jim Hacker was so ludicrously proud.

I told Watson that nobody could see the Minister without an appointment,

[1] In conversation with the Editors.

and left the Private Office to go to the Whips' Office. I was even having to run errands myself, as we were so short-staffed. Had we been fully staffed, Watson would never even have got as far as Hacker's Private Office without an appointment. I left a typist to arrange an appointment for Watson to see Hacker.

Apparently, after I left the room, Brough of Manpower Planning telephoned to say he had missed his train from Newcastle, and could not keep his appointment. Watson overheard, realised that Hacker was free at that moment, and walked straight into his office.

And because there were no other Private Secretaries, due to the economy drive, no one stopped him. And no one warned the Minister that he was meeting Watson instead of Brough.

No greater mishap could have occurred.

December 21st
Today, everything collapsed in ruins. Total disaster.

I was expecting Mr Brough of Manpower Planning (NE Region) at 3.00 p.m. A man walked into my office and naturally I assumed he was Brough.

'Mr Brough?' I said.

'No,' he said, 'my name's Ron Watson. Mr Brough has had to cancel the meeting.'

Naturally, I assumed that Watson had been sent by Brough, and had come instead. So I interrupted, thanked him for coming and asked him to sit down and said, 'Look, Mr Watson, before we start there's one point I have to emphasise. This simply must not get out. If the unions were to hear of this all hell would break loose.'

'I see,' he said.

'Of *course* there are going to be redundancies,' I continued. 'You can't slim down a giant bureaucracy without getting rid of people. Ultimately, lots of people.'

He asked me if I wouldn't be holding discussions with the unions first.

I continued to dig my own grave. 'We'll go through the usual charade of consultation first,' I said, blithely unaware of the impending catastrophe, 'but you know what trades unionists are like. Just bloody-minded, and as thick as two short planks.' How could I have spoken like this to a total stranger?

'All of them?' he asked politely.

I was surprised by this question. I thought he should know, after all, he had to negotiate with them. 'Pretty well,' I said. 'All they're interested in is poaching members from each other or getting themselves on the telly – and they can never keep their big mouths shut.'

I remember quite clearly every word that I spoke. Each one is branded on my heart. Furthermore, it's all written down in front of me – in an interview that Watson gave to the *Standard* as soon as he left my office.

Then the man asked me about drivers and transport service staff, specifically. 'They'll be the first to go,' I said. 'We're wasting a fortune on cars and drivers. And they're all on the fiddle anyway.'

It was at this moment that Watson revealed that he was not Mr Brough's deputy, but was in fact the General Secretary of the Civil Service Transport and Associated Government Workers. And he had come to my office to check that there was no truth in the rumours about redundancies for his members!

Oh my God! . . .

December 23rd

Yesterday and today there has been an acute shortage of Christmas cheer.

All the Civil Service drivers are on strike. I arrived yesterday morning, having read all about the strike in the Press. All the papers quoted Ron Watson quoting me: 'Of course there's going to be redundancies. Lots.'

I asked Bernard how he could have let this happen.

'CBE, Minister,' he replied, unhappily.

I wasn't sure what he meant. Could I have been awarded the CBE? – or could *he*?

He explained. 'Can't Be Everywhere'. Another idiotic Civil Service abbreviation. 'In normal circumstances . . .' he petered out. After all, we both knew how this tragedy had occurred.

Bernard reminded me of all my appointments for today. An office Christmas party, some meetings – nothing of any consequence. I spent the day dodging the Press. I wanted to discuss the situation with Sir Humphrey, but apparently he was unavailable all day.

Annie and I were invited to the French Embassy's Christmas party, at 8.00 p.m. I asked Bernard to get me my car – and then realised, as I spoke, that there were no drivers. I told him to call Annie, to get her to bring our car in to collect me.

Bernard had already thought of that, but apparently our car had been giving trouble all day and Annie wanted to take it to the garage. I got hold of her and told her the garage would wait – the car would get us from Whitehall to Kensington okay.

Annie came for me, we set off in our evening clothes.

Yet again I was wrong and the bloody car broke down in Knightsbridge. In the rush hour. In the pouring rain. I tried to fix it. I was wearing my dinner jacket. I asked Annie for the umbrella, she said I had it. I knew she had it. We shouted at each other, she got out and slammed her door and walked away, and I was left with the car blocking all of Harrods' Christmas rush hour traffic with horns blaring and drivers yelling abuse at me.

I got to the French Embassy an hour and a half late, soaked to the skin and covered in oil. I had three or four glasses of Champagne right away – well, who wouldn't in the circumstances? I needed them!

When I left, not drunk exactly, but a bit the worse for wear, I must admit, I dropped my keys in the gutter beside the car. Then they fell down a grating, so I had to lie down to try and reach them, and some bastard from the Press was there.

This morning I had a frightful hangover. I felt tired and sick. The Press had really gone to town over my alleged drunkenness. They really are unbelievably irresponsible nowadays.

Another paper's headline was HACKER TIRED AND EMOTIONAL AFTER EMBASSY RECEPTION.

Sir Humphrey read it aloud, and remarked that it was slightly better, perhaps, than the first.

'Better?' I asked.

'Well . . . different, anyway,' said Sir Humphrey.

I asked if anyone had said anything beyond, 'tired and emotional'. Bernard informed me that William Hickey said I was 'overwrought'. I didn't mind that quite so much, until Sir Humphrey added – for clarification – 'overwrought as a newt, actually'.

By now I felt that it could not get any worse. But I was wrong. Bernard produced today's lead story from the *Daily Telegraph*, which astonishingly and horrifyingly, claimed that *I* was recruiting extra staff to the DAA.

Hacker recruits 400 new Civil Servants

By our political staff

In a so-called "economy drive", James Hacker, the Minister for Administrative Affairs, has recruited four hundred more Civil Servants.

I demanded an explanation from Sir Humphrey. And he had one ready, of course.

'Minister, you *asked* for these extra people. You demanded a complete study, a survey, facts and figures. These measures cannot be taken by non-people. If you create more work, more people have to be employed to do it. It's common sense.'

While I was taking this on the chin, he came in with another right hook to the head. 'And if you persist with your Bureaucratic Watch-dog Office, there'll be at least another four hundred new jobs there as well.'

I was shattered. My head was aching, I felt sick, my career seemed to be in ruins, I was being pilloried in the Press and the only idea of mine that I've managed to push through since I've been here had now to be abandoned.

Yet, throughout, from my first day here, all the permanent officials appear to have been doing their best to help me in every possible way. So are they completely inept? Or am I? Are they pretending to help while secretly obstructing my every move? Or are they incapable of understanding a new approach to the Department's work? Do they try to help me by pushing me towards the Ministry's policy? Is there a difference between the Minister's policy and the Ministry's policy? Why am I asking so many questions to which there is no known answer? How deep is the ocean, how high is the sky? [*Irving Berlin –* Ed.]

There was silence in the office. I didn't know what we were going to do about the four hundred new people supervising our economy drive or the four hundred new people for the Bureaucratic Watchdog Office, or anything! I simply sat and waited and hoped that my head would stop thumping and that some idea would be suggested by someone sometime soon.

Sir Humphrey obliged. 'Minister . . . if we were to end the economy drive and close the Bureaucratic Watchdog Office we could issue an immediate Press announcement that you had axed eight hundred jobs.' He had obviously thought this out carefully in advance, for at this moment he produced a slim folder from under his arm. 'If you'd like to approve this draft. . . .'

I couldn't believe the impertinence of the suggestion. Axed eight hundred jobs? 'But no one was ever doing these jobs,' I pointed out incredulously. 'No one's been appointed yet.'

'Even greater economy,' he replied instantly. 'We've saved eight hundred redundancy payments as well.'

'But . . .' I attempted to explain '. . . that's just phony. It's dishon-est, it's juggling with figures, it's pulling the wool over people's eyes.'

'A government Press release, in fact,' said Humphrey. I've met some cynical politicians in my time, but this remark from my Perma-nent Secretary was a real eye-opener.

I nodded weakly. Clearly if I was to avoid the calamity of four hundred new people employed to make economies, I had to give up the four hundred new people in my cherished Watch Dog Office. An inevitable *quid pro quo*. After all, politics is the art of the possible. [*A saying generally attributed to R. A. Butler, but actually said by Bismarck (1815–1898) 'Die Politik ist die Lehre von Möglichen' in 1867, in conversation with Meyer von Waldeck – Ed.*]

However, one vital central question, the question that was at the root of this whole debacle, remained completely unanswered. 'But Humphrey,' I said. 'How are we actually going to slim down the Civil Service?'

There was a pause. Then he said: 'Well . . . I suppose we could lose one or two of the tea ladies.'

4

Big
Brother

Nothing of interest happened over Christmas. I spent the week in the constituency. I went to the usual Christmas parties for the constituency party, the old people's home, the general hospital, and assorted other gatherings and it all went off quite well – I got my photo in the local rag four or five times, and avoided saying anything that committed me to anything.

I sensed a sort of resentment, though, and have become aware that I'm in a double-bind situation. The local party, the constituency, my family, *all* of them are proud of me for getting into the Cabinet – yet they are all resentful that I have less time to spend on them and are keen to remind me that I'm nothing special, just their local MP, and that I mustn't get 'too big for my boots'. They manage both to grovel and patronise me simultaneously. It's hard to know how to handle it.

If only I could tell them what life is really like in Whitehall, they would know that there's absolutely no danger of my getting too big for my boots. Sir Humphrey Appleby will see to that.

Back to London today for a TV interview on *Topic*, with Robert McKenzie. He asked me lots of awkward questions about the National Data Base.

We met in the Hospitality Room before the programme was recorded, and I tried to find out what angle he was taking. We were a little tense with each other, of course. [*McKenzie used to call the Hospitality Room the Hostility Room – Ed.*]

'We are going to talk about cutting government extravagance and that sort of thing, aren't we?' I asked, and immediately realised that I had phrased that rather badly.

Bob McKenzie was amused. 'You want to talk about the government's extravagance?' he said with a twinkle in his eye.

'About the ways in which I'm cutting it down, I mean,' I said firmly.

'We'll get to that if we have time after the National Data Base,' he said.

I tried to persuade him that people weren't interested in the Data Base, that it was too trivial. He said he thought people were *very* interested in it, and were worried about Big Brother. This annoyed me, and I told him he couldn't trivialise the National Data Base with that sort of sensationalistic approach. Bob replied that as I'd just said it was trivial already, why not?

We left the Hospitality Room. In the studio, waiting for the programme to begin, a girl with a powder puff kept flitting about and dabbing at my face and preventing me from thinking straight. She said I was getting a bit pink. 'We can't have that,' said Bob jovially, 'what would the *Daily Telegraph* say?'

Just before we started recording I remarked that I could well do without all those old chestnut questions like, 'Are we creating a Police State?'

In retrospect, perhaps this was a mistake.

[*We have found, in the BBC Archives, a complete transcript of Robert McKenzie's interview with James Hacker. It is printed overleaf. – Ed.*]

BRITISH BROADCASTING CORPORATION

TOPIC DECEMBER 30TH INTERVIEW BETWEEN ROBERT MCKENZIE AND THE RT HON JAMES HACKER MP

MCKENZIE: Good evening.   Is Big Brother watching you ?   To be more precise, did you know that the Government is building up a dossier on you ?

It's called by the harmless sounding name of "National Integrated Data Base".   What it means is that at the press of a button any Civil Servant can inspect just about every detail of your life – your tax, your medical record, the car you drive, the house you live in, motoring offences, periods of unemployment, children's school records, the lot – and that Civil Servant may happen to be your next door neighbour.

Recently there has been mounting concern over this powerful totalitarian weapon that the computer revolution has put in the Government's hands.

And the man who wields that weapon is the Minister for Administrative Affairs, the Rt Hon James Hacker MP.

Minister, are you laying the foundations of a police state in this country ?

HACKER: You know, I'm glad you asked me that question.

PAUSE

MCKENZIE: In that case, Minister, could we have an answer ?

BRITISH BROADCASTING CORPORATION

HACKER: (CONT) Yes, of course. I'm about to give you one, if I may. As I was saying, I'm glad you asked me that question. Because ... well, because it's a question that a lot of people are asking. And why ? Because ... well, because a lot of people want to know the answer to it. And let's be quite clear about this - without beating about the bush - the plain fact of the matter is that it is a very important question indeed and people have a right to know.

PAUSE

MCKENZIE: But Minister, you haven't given me an answer yet.

PAUSE

HACKER: I'm sorry, what was the question ?

MCKENZIE: How can I know that if I annoy you in this interview, you won't go back to your office, press a button and examine my tax returns, my hospital records, my police record ...

HACKER: Oh, come on Bob, you know as well as I do that's not the way we do things in this country. Impossible to organise, anyway.

MCKENZIE: Are you saying, Minister, you would like to do those things, but you are too incompetent as yet ?

- 2 -

BRITISH BROADCASTING CORPORATION

HACKER: (CONT) We're not incompetent. We could certainly check up on you if we wanted, that is, er, check up on <u>people</u>. Not you, of course, I don't mean you. But we're not interested in people. Er, that is, when I say we're not interested in people, I don't mean we're not interested in people, of course we are, I mean we're not interested in people <u>in that way</u>, if you know what I mean, in that we would never want to check up on ... people.

MCKENZIE: So what's the Data Base for, if it's not for checking up on people ?

HACKER: You know, <u>that's</u> a very interesting question. (PAUSE)   Look, the point is, people have just been alarmed by one or two silly press articles.   It's a computer, that's all, it's for storing up information and speeding up government business thus avoiding a massive expansion of clerical staff.   Computers are good news.

MCKENZIE: But if you put information into it, you're going to want information out !

HACKER: Not necessarily.

MCKENZIE: So you're spending £25 million to store information you're never going to use ?

HACKER: No - yes - no, well - yes, no, there will be safeguards.

- 3 -

80

BRITISH BROADCASTING CORPORATION

MCKENZIE: (CONT) Such as ?

HACKER: Well, we'll be looking at a whole range of possibilities. But it's a complex and highly technical business, you know.

MCKENZIE: Well, perhaps I can help you. Let me read you an extract from an article written two years ago by the Editor of Reform. I think his name was Jim Hacker. The article was called: "Big Brother and the Not-So-Civil-Service". I quote: "if we are to protect the citizen from Government spying, three measures are urgent. One, no Civil Servant must have access to another department's files without specific signed authorisation from a Minister. Two, unauthorised snooping must be made a criminal offence. And three, every citizen should have the right to inspect his own personal file and get errors corrected." What do you think of those proposals, Mr Hacker ? Alarmist ?

HACKER: No, well, I stand by that, I mean, all these things must happen. Er, in due course.

MCKENZIE: Why not now ?

HACKER: Well, Rome wasn't built in a day. It's under review. But ... well, these things take time you know.

MCKENZIE: Mr Hacker, am I talking to the former Editor of Reform or a Civil Service Spokesman ?

- 4 -

81

BRITISH BROADCASTING CORPORATION

HACKER: (CONT) Well, we haven't talked yet about
the safeguards.   My new Bureaucratic Watch Dog Office, for instance,
and ...

MCKENZIE: Mr Hacker it sounds as if we'll be needing
a whole pack of watchdogs before very long.   Thank you very much.

I thought I'd waffled a bit, but Bob told me I'd stonewalled beautifully. We went back to Hospitality for another New Year's drink. I
congratulated him on finding that old article of mine – a crafty move.
He said that one of his research girls had found it, and asked if I
wanted to meet her. I declined – and said I'd just go back to my office
and have a look at her dossier!

I watched the programme in the evening. I think it was okay. I hope
Sir Humphrey is pleased, anyway.

January 2nd
There was divided opinion in the office this afternoon about my TV
appearance three days ago. The matter came up at a 4 p.m. meeting
with Sir Humphrey, Bernard and Frank Weisel.

Humphrey and Bernard thought I'd been splendid. Dignified and
suitable. But Frank's voice was particularly notable by its silence,
during this chorus of praise. When I asked him what he thought, he
just snorted like a horse. I asked him to translate.

He didn't answer me, but turned to Sir Humphrey. 'I congratulate
you,' he began, his manner even a little less charming than usual. 'Jim
is now perfectly house-trained.' Humphrey attempted to excuse himself and leave the room.

'If you'll excuse me, Mr Weasel . . .'

'Weisel!' snapped Frank. He turned on me. 'Do you realise you just
say everything the Civil Service programmes you to say. What are
you, a man or a mouth?'

Nobody laughed at his little pun.

'It may be very hard for a political adviser to understand,' said Sir
Humphrey, in his most patronising manner, 'but I am merely a civil
servant and I just do as I am instructed by my master.'

Frank fumed away, muttering, 'your master, typical stupid bloody
phrase, public school nonsense,' and so forth. I must say, the phrase
interested me too.

'What happens,' I asked, 'if the Minister is a woman? What do you
call her?'

Humphrey was immediately in his element. He loves answering
questions about good form and protocol. 'Yes, that's most interesting. We sought an answer to the point when I was a Principal Private
Secretary and Dr Edith Summerskill was appointed Minister in 1947.
I didn't quite like to refer to her as my mistress.'

He paused. For effect, I thought at first, but then he appeared to
have more to say on the subject.

'What was the answer?' I asked.

'We're still waiting for it,' he explained.

Frank chipped in with a little of his heavy duty irony. 'It's under review is it? Rome wasn't built in a day, eh Sir Humphrey? These things take time, do they?'

Frank is actually beginning to get on my nerves. The chip on his shoulder about the Civil Service is getting larger every day. I don't know why, because they have given him an office, he has free access to me, and they tell me that they give him all possible papers that would be of use to him. Now he's started to take out his aggressions on me. He's like a bear with a sore head. Perhaps he's still getting over his New Year's hangover.

Humphrey wanted to leave, so did I, but Bernard started to give me my diary appointments – and that started another wrangle. Bernard told me I was to meet him at Paddington at 8 a.m. tomorrow, because I was to speak at the Luncheon of the Conference of Municipal Treasurers at the Vehicle Licensing Centre in Swansea. Frank then reminded me that I was due in Newcastle tomorrow night to address the by-election meeting. Bernard pointed out to me that I couldn't do both and I explained this to Frank. Frank pointed out that the by-election was important to us, whereas the Swansea trip was just a Civil Service junket, and I explained this to Bernard. Bernard then reminded me that the Conference had been in my diary for some time and that they all expected me to go to Swansea, and I explained this to Frank and then Frank reminded me that Central House [*the Party Headquarters – Ed.*] expected me to go to Newcastle, but I didn't explain this to Bernard because by this time I was tired of explaining and I said so. So Frank asked Bernard to explain why I was double booked, Bernard said no one had told him about Newcastle, I asked Frank why he hadn't told Bernard, Frank asked me why *I* hadn't told Bernard, and I pointed out that I couldn't remember everything.

'I shall go to Swansea,' I said.

'Is that a decision, Minister?' asked Bernard.

'That's final,' I said.

Frank then played his trump card. 'The PM expects you to go to Newcastle,' he said. Why hadn't he said this till now, stupid man? I asked if he was sure. He nodded.

'Bernard, I think I'd better go to Newcastle,' I said.

'Is that a decision?' asked Frank.

'Yes, that's final,' I said. 'And now I'm going home.'

'Is *that* a decision?' asked Sir Humphrey. I wasn't sure whether or not he was asking for clarification or sending me up. I still find him completely inscrutable. Anyway, he continued: 'Minister, I think you've made the wrong decision, if I may say so. Your visit to Swansea is in the programme, it's been announced, you can't really get out of it.'

This was becoming impossible. They all seem to expect me to be in two places at once. I told them to find some way of getting me from Swansea to Newcastle – train, car, helicopter, I didn't care how – and I would fulfill both engagements. 'And now,' I announced 'I'm going home – that's final!'

'Finally final?' asked Bernard.

He's equally inscrutable.

As I left, Bernard gave Roy, my driver, four red boxes and asked me to be sure to do them tonight because of all the Committee papers for tomorrow and letters that have to go off before the weekend.

'And if you're a good boy,' said Frank in a rather poor imitation of Bernard's accent, 'your nanny will give you a sweetie.'

I really don't have to put up with all this aggravation from Frank. I'm stuck with these damn permanent officials, but Frank is only there at my express invitation. I may have to remind him of this, very soon.

When I got home Annie was packing. 'Leaving me at last?' I enquired jovially. She reminded me that it is our anniversary tomorrow and we have arranged to go to Paris.

I was appalled!

I tried to explain to her about the trips to Swansea and Newcastle. She feels that she doesn't want to spend her anniversary in Swansea and Newcastle, particularly not at a lunch for Municipal Treasurers at the Vehicle Licensing Centre. I can see her point. She told me to cancel my meetings, I said I couldn't, so she said she'd go to Paris without me.

So I phoned Bernard. I told him it was my wife's wedding anniversary – Annie said, 'yours too' – and mine too. Bernard made some silly joke about a coincidence. I told him I was going to Paris tomorrow, instead, and that it was final and that I knew I'd said it was final before but now this was really final – I told him he'd have to sort everything out. Then *he* talked for three minutes and when I rang off I was still going to Swansea and Newcastle tomorrow.

Those civil servants can talk you in or out of anything. I just don't seem to know my own mind any more.

Annie and I fumed in silence for a while, and finally I asked her the really important question of the day: had she seen me on my TV interview – (I'd been in London, she'd been down in the constituency).

'I saw someone who looked like you.'

I asked her what that was supposed to mean. She didn't answer.

'Frank said that I'm just a Civil Service mouthpiece,' I muttered resentfully.

Annie said, 'Yes.'

I was shocked. 'You mean . . . you agree?'

'Of course,' she said. 'You could have hired an actor to say it all for you. He'd have said it better. And while you're at it, why not just sign your letters with a rubber stamp or get an Assistant Secretary to sign them – they write them anyway.'

I tried to remain dignified. 'Assistant Secretaries do not write my letters,' I said. 'Under Secretaries write them.'

'I rest my case, m'lud,' she said.

'You think I've become a puppet too?'

'I do. Maybe they should get Miss Piggy to do your job. At least she's prettier.'

I must say I was feeling pretty hurt and defeated. I sighed and sat on the bed. I honestly felt near to tears. Is this how a Cabinet Minister usually feels, I wondered, or am I just an abysmal failure? I couldn't see what was wrong, but something certainly was.

'I don't know what to do about it,' I said quietly. 'I'm just swamped by the volume of work. I'm so depressed.'

Annie suggested that, as we weren't going to Paris after all, we might at least go for a quiet little candlelit dinner on the corner. I told her that I couldn't, because Bernard had told me to work through three red boxes tonight.

Annie said something which changed my whole perception of my situation. She said, 'What do you mean, "Bernard's told me!"? When you edited *Reform* you were quite different – you went in, you told people what to do, demanded what you wanted, and you got it! What's changed? You're the same man – you're just allowing them to walk all over you.'

And, suddenly, I saw that it was true. She's right. That's why Frank has been getting at me too. Either I get them by the throat or they'll get me by the throat! It's the law of the jungle, just like in the Cabinet.

'How many articles did you blue-pencil and tear up in those days?' she asked.

'Dozens,' I remembered.

'And how many official papers have you torn up?'

'None,' I told her. 'I'm not allowed to.'

She smiled reproachfully at me, and I realised that I still hadn't broken out of this destructive pattern of behaviour.

'Not allowed to?' She held my hand. 'Darling, you're the Minister. You can do anything you like.'

She's right. I am. I can. And, somehow, all my officials have housetrained me. I see it now. Honestly I'm so grateful to Annie, she has such remarkable common sense. Well, they're going to get quite a surprise. Suddenly, I can't wait to get to the office. My New Year Resolution is to Take Charge.

January 4th

Today was better.

But only a little better. *My* attitude was fine, but unfortunately *his* didn't seem to change all that much.

I summoned Humphrey to my office. I don't think he liked being summoned. Then I told him that Frank was absolutely correct, and Bob McKenzie too – the National Data Base has to be organised differently.

To my surprise, he agreed meekly. 'Yes Minister,' he murmured.

'We are going to have all possible built-in safeguards,' I went on.

'Yes Minister,' he murmured again.

'Right away,' I added. This took him by surprise.

'Er . . . what precisely do you mean, right away?'

'I mean right away,' I said.

'Oh I see, you mean *right away*, Minister.'

'Got it in one, Humphrey.'

So far, so good. But, having totally accepted at the start of the conversation that it was all to be different, he now started to chip away at my resolve.

'The only thing is,' he began, 'perhaps I should remind you that we are still in the early months of this government and there's an awful lot to get on with, Minister . . .'

I interrupted. 'Humphrey,' I reiterated firmly, 'we are changing the rules of the Data Base. Now!'

'But you can't, Minister,' he said, coming out into the open.

'I can,' I said, remembering my stern talk from Annie last night, 'I'm the Minister.'

He changed tactics again. 'Indeed you are, Minister,' he said, rapidly switching from bullying to grovelling, 'and quite an excellent

Minister at that, if I may say so.'

I brushed all the flannel aside. 'Never mind the soft soap, Humphrey,' I replied. 'I want all citizens to have the right to check their own file, and I want legislation to make unauthorised access to personal files illegal.'

'Very well,' said Sir Humphrey. 'It shall be done.'

This rather took the wind out of my sails. 'Right,' I said. 'Good,' I said. 'Then we go ahead,' I said, wondering what the catch was.

I was right. There was a catch. Sir Humphrey took this opportunity to explain to me that we can go ahead, if the Cabinet agrees, and take the matter to the Ministerial Committee, and then we can go ahead to the Official Committee. After that, of course, it's all plain sailing – straight to the Cabinet Committee! And then back to Cabinet itself. I interrupted to point out that we'd *started* with Cabinet.

'Only the policy, Minister,' explained Sir Humphrey. 'At this juncture Cabinet will have to consider the specific proposals.'

I conceded the point, but remarked that after going back to Cabinet we could then go ahead. Sir Humphrey agreed – but with the proviso that if Cabinet raises any questions, which it almost certainly would, the proposals would then have to go back to the Ministerial Committee, the Official Committee, the Cabinet Committee and the Cabinet again.

'I know all this,' I said brusquely. 'I'm assuming that Cabinet will raise no objections.' Sir Humphrey raised his eyebrows and visibly refrained from comment.

I didn't know all this at all, actually – the complex mechanics of passing legislation don't ever really become clear to you in Opposition or on the back benches.

'So after Cabinet, we go ahead. Right?'

'Yes,' he said, 'to the Leader of the House Committee. And then to Parliament – where there's the Committee stage of course.'

But suddenly the penny dropped. Suddenly I realised he was blurring the whole issue. A blindfold dropped away from my eyes, as if by magic. 'Humphrey,' I said, 'you're talking about legislation – but *I'm* talking about administrative and procedural changes.'

Sir Humphrey smiled complacently. 'If members of the public are to have the right to take legal action, then legislation is necessary and it will be very complicated.'

I had the answer to that. 'Legislation is not necessary in order for the citizen to be able to see his own file, is it?'

Sir Humphrey thought carefully about this. 'No-o-o-o,' he finally said, with great reluctance.

'Then we'll go ahead with that.' Round one to me, I thought.

But Sir Humphrey had not yet conceded even that much. 'Minister,' he began, 'we could manage that *slightly* quicker, but there are an awful lot of administrative problems as well.'

'Look,' I said, 'this must have come up before. This Data Base has been in preparation for years, it hasn't just materialised overnight – these problems must have been discussed.'

'Yes indeed,' he agreed.

'So what conclusions have been reached?' I asked.

Sir Humphrey didn't reply. At first I thought he was thinking. Then I thought he hadn't heard me, for some curious reason. So I asked him again: 'What conclusions have been reached?' a little louder, just in case. Again there was no visible reaction. I thought he'd become ill.

'Humphrey,' I asked, becoming a little concerned for his health and sanity, 'can you hear me?'

'My lips are sealed,' he replied, through unsealed lips.

I asked him what exactly he meant.

'I am not at liberty to discuss the previous government's plans,' he said. I was baffled.

'Why not?' I asked.

'Minister – would you like everything that you have said and done in the privacy of this office to be revealed subsequently to one of your opponents?'

I'd never thought of that. Of course, I'd be absolutely horrified. It would be a constant threat. I would never be able to speak freely in my own office.

Sir Humphrey knew that he'd scored a bullseye. He pressed home his advantage. 'We cannot give your political opponents ammunition against you – nor vice versa.'

Of course, I can see his point but there is one essential difference in this instance. I pointed out to Sir Humphrey that Tom Sargent was my predecessor, and he wouldn't mind. He's a very decent chap. After all, the Data Base is not a party political matter, politicians of all parties are united on this.

But Sir Humphrey wouldn't budge. 'It's the principle, Minister,' he said, and added that it just wouldn't be cricket.

This was a powerful argument. Naturally I don't want to do anything that's not cricket. So I suppose I'll never know what went on before I came here. I can't see a way round that.

So where have we got to? We've established that we don't need legislation to enable the citizen to see his own file, but that there are numerous unspecified admin. problems that have to be solved first.

One other thing occurred today. Bernard said that because of the adverse (Bernard called it 'not entirely favourable') Press reaction to my appearance on *Topic*, the other network wants me to appear on their programme *World in Focus*. Funny how television is never interested when you've got an important announcement to make, but the moment some trivial thing goes wrong the phone never stops ringing. At first I told him to decline, but he said that if I don't appear they'll do the item anyway, and no one will be there to state my case.

I asked Humphrey what I was to say about safeguards for the Data Base, in view of our very limited progress today. 'Perhaps you could remind them, Minister, that Rome wasn't built in a day.'

Big help.

As I review the meeting, writing it all down for this diary, I now feel that I got absolutely nowhere today. But there must be *some* way to get Sir Humphrey and the DAA to do what I tell them.

[*In the light of Hacker's experience and frustrations, it is as well to remember that if a Whitehall committee is not positively stopped, it will continue. There could be a Crimea committee, for all we know. There is very probably a ration-book committee and an identity-card committee. – Ed.*]

January 6th

Today, by a lucky chance, I learned a bit more about dealing with Sir Humphrey.

I bumped into Tom Sargent, in the House of Commons smoking room. I asked if I could join him, and he was only too pleased.

'How are you enjoying being in Opposition?' I asked him jocularly.

Like the good politician he is, he didn't exactly answer my question. 'How are you enjoying being in government?' he replied.

I could see no reason to beat about the bush, and I told him that, quite honestly, I'm not enjoying it as much as I'd expected to.

'Humphrey got you under control?' he smiled.

I dodged that one, but said that it's so very hard to get anything done. He nodded, so I asked him, 'did *you* get anything done?'

'Almost nothing,' he replied cheerfully. 'But I didn't cotton on to his technique till I'd been there over a year – and then of course there was the election.'

It emerged from the conversation that the technique in question was Humphrey's system for stalling.

According to Tom, it's in five stages. I made a note during our conversation, for future reference.

Stage One: Humphrey will say that the administration is in its early months and there's an awful lot of other things to get on with. (Tom clearly knows his stuff. That is just what Humphrey said to me the day before yesterday.)

Stage Two: If I persist past Stage One, he'll say that he quite appreciates the intention, something certainly ought to be done – but is this the right way to achieve it?

Stage Three: If I'm still undeterred he will shift his ground from how I do it to *when* I do it, i.e. 'Minister, this is not the time, for all sorts of reasons.'

Stage Four: Lots of Ministers settle for Stage Three according to Tom. But if not, he will then say that the policy has run into difficulties – technical, political and/or legal. (Legal difficulties are best because they can be made totally incomprehensible and can go on for ever.)

Stage Five: Finally, because the first four stages have taken up to three years, the last stage is to say that, 'we're getting rather near to the run up to the next general election – so we can't be sure of getting the policy through.'

The stages can be made to last three years because at each stage Sir Humphrey will do absolutely nothing until the Minister chases him. And he assumes, rightly, that the Minister has too much else to do. [*The whole process is called Creative Inertia – Ed.*]

Tom asked me what the policy was that I'm trying to push through. When I told him that I'm trying to make the National Integrated Data Base less of a Big Brother, he roared with laughter.

'I suppose he's pretending it's all new?'

I nodded.

'Clever old sod,' said Tom, 'we spent years on that. We almost had a White Paper ready to bring out, but the election was called. I've done it all.'

I could hardly believe my ears. I asked about the administrative problems. Tom said there were none – all solved. And Tom guessed that my enquiries about the past were met with silence – 'clever bugger, he's wiped the slate clean.'

Anyway, now I know the five stages, I should be able to deal with Humphrey quite differently. Tom advised me not to let on that we'd had this conversation, because it would spoil the fun. He also warned me of the 'Three Varieties of Civil Service Silence', which would be Humphrey's last resort if completely cornered:

1 The silence when they do not want to tell you the facts: *Discreet Silence.*
2 The silence when they do not intend to take any action: *Stubborn Silence.*
3 The silence when you catch them out and they haven't a leg to stand on. They imply that they could vindicate themselves completely if only they were free to tell all, but they are too honourable to do so: *Courageous Silence.*

Finally Tom told me what Humphrey's next move would be. He asked how many boxes they'd given me for tonight: 'Three? Four?'

'Five,' I admitted, somewhat shamefaced.

'Five?' He couldn't hide his astonishment at how badly I was doing. 'Have they told you that you needn't worry too much about the fifth?' I nodded. 'Right. Well, I'll bet you that at the bottom of the fifth box will be a submission explaining why any new moves on the Data Base must be delayed – and if you never find it or read it they'll do nothing further, and in six months' time they'll say they told you all about it.'

There was one more thing I wanted to ask Tom, who really had been extremely kind and helpful. He's been in office for years, in various government posts. So I said to him: 'Look Tom, you know all the Civil Service tricks.'

'Not all,' he grinned, 'just a few hundred.'

'Right,' I said. 'Now how do you defeat them? How do you make them do something they do not want to do?'

Tom smiled ruefully, and shook his head. 'My dear fellow,' he replied, 'if I knew that I wouldn't be in Opposition.'

January 7th

I did my boxes so late last night that I'm writing up yesterday's discoveries a day late.

Tom had been most helpful to me. When I got home I told Annie all about it over dinner. She couldn't understand why Tom, as a member of the Opposition, would have been so helpful.

I explained to her that the Opposition aren't really the opposition. They're just called the Opposition. But, in fact, they are the opposition in exile. The Civil Service are the opposition in residence.

Then after dinner I did the boxes and sure enough, at the bottom of the fifth box, I found a submission on the Data Base. Not merely at the bottom of the fifth box – to be doubly certain the submission had somehow slipped into the middle of an eighty-page report on Welfare Procedures.

By the way, Tom has also lent me all his private papers on the Data Base, which he kept when he left office. V. useful!

The submission contained the expected delaying phrases: 'Subject still under discussion . . . programme not finalised . . . nothing precipitate . . . failing instructions to the contrary propose await developments.'

Annie suggested I ring Humphrey and tell him that I disagree. I was reluctant – it was 2 a.m., and he'd be fast asleep.

'Why should he sleep while you're working?' Annie asked me. 'After all, he's had you on the run for three months. Now it's your turn.'

'I couldn't possibly do that,' I said.

Annie looked at me. 'What's his number?' I asked, as I reached for our address book.

Annie added reasonably: 'After all, if it was in the fifth box you couldn't have found it any earlier, could you?'

Humphrey answered the phone with a curious sort of grunting noise. I had obviously woken him up. 'Sorry to ring you so late, you weren't in the middle of dinner, were you?'

'No,' he said, sounding somewhat confused, 'we had dinner some while ago. What's the time?'

I told him it was 2 a.m.

'Good God!' He sounded as though he'd really woken up now. 'What's the crisis?'

'No crisis. I'm still going through my red boxes and I knew you'd still be hard at it.'

'Oh yes,' he said, stifling a yawn. 'Nose to the grindstone.'

I told him I'd just got to the paper on the Data Base.

'Oh, you've found . . .' he corrected himself without pausing, 'you've read it.'

I told him that I thought he needed to know, straight away, that I wasn't happy with it, that I knew he'd be grateful to have a little extra time to work on something else, and that I hoped he didn't mind my calling him.

'Always a pleasure to hear from you, Minister,' he said, and I think he slammed down the phone.

After I rang off I realised I'd forgotten to tell him to come and talk about it before Cabinet tomorrow. I was about to pick up the phone when Annie said: 'Don't ring him now.'

I was surprised by this sudden show of kindness and consideration for Sir Humphrey, but I agreed. 'No, perhaps it is a bit late.'

She smiled. 'Yes. Just give him another ten minutes.'

January 8th

This morning I made a little more progress in my battle for control over Humphrey and my Department, though the battle is not yet won.

But I had with me my notes from the meeting with Tom Sargent, and – exactly as Tom had predicted – Sir Humphrey put his stalling technique into bat.

'Humphrey,' I began, 'have you drafted the proposed safeguards for the Data Base?'

'Minister,' he replied plausibly, 'I quite appreciate your intention and I fully agree that there is a need for safeguards but I'm wondering if this is the right way to achieve it.'

'It's my way,' I said decisively, and I ticked off the first objection in my little notebook. 'And that's my decision.'

Humphrey was surprised that his objection had been brushed aside so early, without protracted discussion – so surprised that he went straight on to his second stage.

'Even so Minister,' he said, 'this is not really the time, for all sorts of reasons.'

I ticked off number two in my notebook, and replied: 'It is the perfect time – safeguards have to develop parallel with systems, not after them – that's common sense.'

Humphrey was forced to move on to his third objection. Tom really has analysed his technique well.

'Unfortunately Minister,' said Humphrey doggedly, 'we have tried this before, but, well . . . we have run into all sorts of difficulties.'

I ticked off number three in my little book. Humphrey had noticed this by now, and tried to look over my shoulder to see what was written there. I held the book away from him.

'What sort of difficulties?' I enquired.

'Technical, for example,' said Humphrey.

Thanks to a careful study of Tom's private papers, I had the answer ready. 'No problem at all,' I said airily. 'I've been doing some research. We can use the same basic file interrogation programme as the US State Department and the Swedish Ministry of the Interior. No technical problems.'

Sir Humphrey was getting visibly rattled, but he persisted. 'There are also formidable administrative problems. All departments are affected. An inter-departmental committee will have to be set up . . .'

I interrupted him in mid-sentence. 'No,' I said firmly. 'I think you'll find, if you look into it, that the existing security procedures are adequate. This can just be an extension. Anything else?'

Humphrey was gazing at me with astonishment. He just couldn't work out how I was so thoroughly in command of the situation. Was I just making a series of inspired guesses, he wondered. As he didn't speak for a moment, I decided to help him out.

'Legal problems?' I suggested helpfully.

'Yes Minister,' he agreed at once, hoping that he had me cornered at last. Legal problems were always his best bet.

'Good, good,' I said, and ticked off the last but one stage on my little list. Again he tried to see what I had written down.

'There is a question,' he began carefully, 'of whether we have the legal power . . .'

'I'll answer it,' I announced grandly. 'We have.' He was looking at me in wonderment. 'All personnel affected are bound by their service agreement anyway.'

He couldn't argue because, of course, I was right. Grasping at straws he said: 'But Minister, there will have to be extra staffing – are you sure you will get it through Cabinet and the Parliamentary Party?'

'Quite sure,' I said. 'Anything else?' I looked at my list. 'No nothing else. Right, so we go ahead?'

Humphrey was silent. I wondered whether he was being discreet, stubborn or courageous. Stubborn, I think.

Eventually, *I* spoke. 'You're very silent,' I remarked. There was more silence. 'Why are you so silent, by the way?'

He realised that he had to speak, or the jig was up. 'Minister, you do not seem to realise how much work is involved.'

Casually, I enquired if he'd never investigated safeguards before, under another government perhaps, as I thought I remembered written answers to Parliamentary questions in the past.

His reply went rather as follows: 'Minister, in the first place, we've agreed that the question is not cricket. In the second place, if there had been investigations, which there haven't or not necessarily, or I am not at liberty to say if there have, there would have been a project team which, had it existed, on which I cannot comment, would now be disbanded if it had existed and the members returned to their original departments, had there indeed been any such members.' Or words to that effect.

I waited till the torrent of useless language came to a halt, and then

I delivered my ultimatum. I told him that I wanted safeguards on the use of the Data Base made available immediately. He told me it isn't possible. I told him it is. He told me it isn't. I told him it is. We went on like that ('tis, 'tisn't, 'tis, 'tisn't) like a couple of three-year-olds, glowering at each other, till Bernard popped in.

I didn't want to reveal that Tom had told me of the safeguards that were ready and waiting, because then I'd have no more aces up my sleeve.

While I contemplated this knotty problem, Bernard reminded me of my engagements: Cabinet at 10.00, a speech to the Anglo-American Society lunch, and the *World in Focus* interview this evening. I asked him if he could get me out of the lunch. 'Not really, Minister,' he answered, 'it's been announced. It's in the programme.'

And suddenly the penny dropped. The most wonderful plan formed in my mind, the idea of the century!

I told Humphrey and Bernard to be sure to watch me on TV tonight.

[*The transcript of Hacker's appearance that night on* World in Focus *follows. It contains his first truly memorable victory over his officials–Ed.*]

THIS IS AN UNCORRECTED TRANSCRIPT ONLY.   NOT FOR
CIRCULATION WITHOUT PROGRAMME CONTROLLER'S APPROVAL.

WORLD IN FOCUS – JANUARY 8 – HACKER INTERVIEW

PRESENTER   And our man on the spot tonight
is the Right Honourable Jim Hacker, Minister for Administrative Affairs, and the man at the heart of the Big
Brother computer controversy.   He's talking to Godfrey
Finch.

FINCH   Minister, as you know, there's been an
outcry this week about the dossier that the Civil Service
Bureaucracy is apparently starting to build up on every
citizen in the country.   It is rumoured that this is not
your own policy, that you wish to have safeguards for the
individual citizen, but that you are being totally frustrated
every step of the way by the Civil Service machine.

HACKER   You know Godfrey, there's a lot of
nonsense talked about the Civil Service.   It is actually
a marvellous, efficient, professional organisation
capable of tremendous effort and speed.   It is full of
talented, dedicated people who do all they can to help
Government policies become law.

FINCH   Thank you for the commercial, Minister.
If we could start the programme now ?

HACKER   The fact is, the Civil Service and I are in complete accord on this whole matter, and our proposals are now ready for publication.

I am happy to announce tonight that, from March 1st, every citizen of the UK will have the absolute right to inspect his personal file and to check any information that he or she has ever supplied to the Government.

Secondly, no Civil Servant will be allowed to examine personal files from another department without written authority from a Minister.   And I shall be announcing, in the House next week, legislation enabling the citizens to take legal action against any Civil Servant who gains unauthorised access to his file.

FINCH   Well ... that's, er ... well, that's very interesting and encouraging, Minister.   Why did you not say so earlier and put people's minds at rest ?

HACKER   Frankly, Godfrey, I didn't believe the Civil Service could meet those deadlines.   But they've convinced me that they can.   Indeed my Permanent Secretary is staking his reputation on it.

And, if not, heads will roll.

Jim Hacker always gave me the credit for this brilliant ploy, because of the unintentional double meaning of my remark, 'it's been announced, it's in the programme.'

However, I personally believe that Hacker was inspired by Edward Heath's famous manoeuvre when he was Prime Minister and wanted – in the teeth of Civil Service opposition – to announce a new £10 Christmas bonus for the Old Age Pensioners. After many weeks of obstruction within Number Ten he simply appeared on *Panorama* and announced it as a *fait accompli*. It happened. It happened late, but it happened.

I well remember that Humphrey Appleby's face was a picture when Jim made his statement – especially at the moment when he said that his Permanent Secretary had staked his reputation on it.

He turned to me and said: 'It can't be done.' I made no reply.

Then he said to me: 'Well Bernard, what do you make of the Minister's performance?'

I was obliged to say that, in my opinion, it was checkmate.

January 9th

Today was my happiest day since I became a Minister.

'Did you see me on the box last night?' I asked Humphrey cheerfully as he gloomed into the office looking like Mr Sowerberry at a funeral.

'Of course,' he replied, tight-lipped.

Actually, it didn't matter whether he'd seen me or not, because my TV appearance was completely reported in this morning's Press.

'How was I?' I asked innocently, 'Good?'

'A most remarkable performance, Minister, if I may say so,' he answered with studied ambiguity.

'You may, you may,' I said, affecting not to notice it.

'Minister, we have been working very hard all night, and I'm happy to be able to inform you that we have come up with some draft proposals that would enable you to achieve your desired objectives by the stated dates.'

In other words, he spent five minutes digging out from the files the proposals agreed last year when Tom was Minister.

'Well done, Humphrey,' I said ingenuously. 'You see, I told the nation how splendid you are and I was right. I had every confidence in you.'

'Quite so, Minister,' he said through clenched teeth.

---

[1] In conversation with the Editors.

He got out a folder containing his proposals.

'Are those your proposals?' I asked.

'Yes.'

'Here are mine,' I said, and produced a folder too.

'You have proposals too?' He was surprised.

I told Humphrey to read his proposed safeguards. Then I would read mine. And we would see how they compared.

Humphrey started reading. 'One – Personal Data – 1A. Safeguards must be applied with reference to . . .'

I could resist it no longer. Reading from my folder, I joined in, and together, in unison, we read: 'Two – criteria – the need to know and the right to know. 1.A(i) the need to know. Only those officials for whom the information was submitted may be deemed, *prima facie*, to have a need to know.'

We looked at each other.

'We seem to be of the same mind,' I remarked.

'Where did those proposals come from?' he demanded. I said nothing. After a few moments he repeated, 'where did those proposals come from?'

'Humphrey,' I replied in a tone of slight reproof, 'my lips are sealed.'

5

The Writing on the Wall

The help that I received from Tom Sargent in the matter of the National Data Base might seem unusual to those who are outside the extraordinary world of politics. Strange though it may seem to those members of the public who read numerous abusive speeches in which members of the two main political parties revile each other as incompetent, dishonest, criminally stupid and negligent, cross-party friendships are extremely common. In fact, it is much easier to be friends with a member of the opposite party than a member of one's own party – for one is not in direct personal competition for office with members of the Opposition in the way that one is with one's colleagues.

All my Cabinet colleagues and I were naturally in bitter competition with each other during our years in Opposition. In the last three months we've all been so busy trying to deal with the *real* opposition – the Civil Service – that we've not had any real time to do-down each other. But I have a hunch, from the recent atmosphere in Cabinet, that some political manoeuvring is in the air again.

There are still numerous other matters concerning me, about which I have also had a little time to reflect this weekend. I realised early on (in my first week as a Minister, in fact) that Open Government presents real problems. It was made clear to me that if people stop having secrets they stop having power.

In fact, paradoxically, government is more open when it is less open. Open Government is rather like the live theatre: the audience gets a performance. And it gives a response. But, like the theatre, in order to have something to show openly there must first be much hidden activity. And all sorts of things have to be cut or altered in rehearsals, and not shown to the public until you have got them right.

The drawback with all this is that it begs the question – which is that

101

the Civil Service keeps secrets from Ministers. They say they don't, but I'm sure they do. I'm now all in favour of keeping secrets from the public of course, for the reasons I've just given, but it should be *my* privilege, as the people's elected representative, to decide when to keep the people in ignorance. It should not be up to the Civil Service to keep *me* in ignorance.

Unfortunately, it is pretty hard to get this across to them.

I have also learned a few general lessons. I must never show my hopes or fears to Humphrey, if I can avoid it – especially Party fears. If you give away your political weaknesses, they'll destroy you. You have to keep them guessing.

I now realise that I should always get civil servants to commit themselves first. Never say, 'I think . . .', but always say, 'What do *you* think . . .?'

I've also learned about 'yes' and 'no'. You can always turn a 'no' into a 'yes' – but not vice versa. Furthermore, when you say 'no', let the Private Office say it for you – but when you say 'yes', pre-empt the Private Office and phone up yourself. That way, *they* get the blame and *I* get the credit.

In fact, the point about making your own phone calls is crucial. The whole system is designed to prevent you from doing anything your-self. As far as the Civil Service is concerned, you must never make a phone call, or sort out a problem. Woe betide any Minister who lifts the phone to try to sort out a foreign trade deal, for instance. Civil servants will come at you from all sides mouthing phrases like, 'it's an FCO matter . . . correct channels . . . policy hangs by a thread . . . you *do* realise, don't you? . . . what if something were to go wrong? . . . on your head be it, Minister!' and many others.

This is all very squashing to the morale of an important public figure such as myself. If you're not careful they'll eventually have you in such a state that you'll be frightened to phone Potters Bar.

Furthermore, everything that one does is carefully watched and supervised. Bernard listens in to all my phone calls, except the ones that I make on the private line. The theory is that he can make useful notes on my behalf, and is fully informed about my views and activities – true! But, as we know, information is a double-edged sword. [*It's no accident that most of the really powerful offices in the world are called 'Secretary' – Secretary of State, Permanent Secretary, General Secretary, Party Secretary, etc. 'Secretary' means the person who is entrusted with the secrets, the information no one else knows – the élite. – Ed.*]

102

I must say, though, that I find it an invaluable way to pass on criticism of my permanent officials, knowing that Bernard is listening in to my every word!

Tonight, in one of my red boxes, there is a third redraft of a report to the Think-Tank on Civil Service overmanning. ['*Think-Tank*' *was the colloquial name of the Central Policy Review Staff – Ed.*] I'm still not pleased with it. I shall have a lot of questions to ask about it tomorrow morning.

January 11th

We had a meeting about the Think-Tank report. I told Humphrey that I still wasn't happy with it, and he obligingly offered to redraft it.

This hardly seems to be the answer. I pointed out that he had redrafted it three times already.

Bernard argued about this. 'That's not quite correct, Minister.'

I told him I could count. And that this was the third draft. 'Quite so,' he said. 'It has been drafted once and redrafted twice.' A typical piece of boring pedantic quibbling. Bernard has an idiotic obsession about using language with accuracy – it's fortunate he's not in politics.

I told him not to quibble, and Humphrey said placatingly he would be happy to redraft the report a third time. Of course he would. And a fourth time, and a fifth no doubt. 'And a sixth,' I went on. 'But it still won't say what *I* want it to say, it will say what *you* want it to say. And I want it to say what *I* want it to say.'

'What do you want it to say?' asked Bernard.

'We want it to say what you want it to say,' murmured Humphrey soothingly.

'I'm sure,' wittered Bernard, 'that the Department doesn't want you to say something that you don't want to say.'

I tried again. For the fourth time in as many weeks I explained the position. 'Six weeks ago the Think-Tank asked for our evidence on Civil Service overmanning. Three times I have briefed a group of civil servants in words of one syllable – and each time I get back a totally unintelligible draft which says the exact opposite of what I have told them to say.'

'With respect, Minister,' countered Sir Humphrey (untruthfully), 'how do you know it says the opposite if it is totally unintelligible?' He really is the master of the irrelevant question-begging answer.

'All I want to say,' I explained plaintively, 'is that the Civil Service is grossly overmanned and must be slimmed down.'

'I'm sure we all want to say that,' lied my Permanent Secretary.

'And that is what the report says.'

'No it doesn't.'

'Yes it does.'

Then we said, 'Oh no, it doesn't', 'Oh yes, it does,' 'Oh no, it doesn't,' at each other for a while. Then I quoted phrases from the draft report at him. It says, for instance, that a phased reduction of about a hundred thousand people is 'not in the public interest'. Translation: it *is* in the public interest but it is not in the interest of the Civil Service. 'Public opinion is not yet ready for such a step,' it says. Translation: Public opinion is ready but the Civil Service is not! Then it goes on: 'However, this is an urgent problem and we therefore propose setting up a Royal Commission.' Translation: This problem is a bloody nuisance, but we hope that by the time a Royal Commission reports, four years from now, everyone will have forgotten about it or we can find someone else to blame.

[*Hacker was beginning to understand Civil Service code language. Other examples are:*

'I think we have to be very careful.' Translation: We are not going to do this.

'Have you thought through all the implications?' Translation: You are not going to do this.

'It is a slightly puzzling decision.' Translation: Idiotic!

'Not entirely straightforward.' Translation: Criminal.

'With the greatest possible respect, Minister . . .' Translation: Minister, that is the silliest idea I've ever heard. – Ed.]

Humphrey could see no way out of this impasse. 'Minister, I can only suggest that we redraft it.' Brilliant!

'Humphrey,' I said, 'will you give me a straight answer to a straight question?'

This question took him completely by surprise, and he stopped to think for a brief moment.

'So long as you are not asking me to resort to crude generalisations or vulgar over-simplifications, such as a simple yes or no,' he said, in a manner that contrived to be both openly ingenuous and deeply evasive, 'I shall do my utmost to oblige.'

'Do you mean yes?' I asked.

A fierce internal struggle appeared to be raging within. 'Yes,' he said finally.

'Right,' I said. 'Here is the straight question.'

Sir Humphrey's face fell. 'Oh,' he said, 'I thought that was it.'

I persevered. 'Humphrey, in your evidence to the Think-Tank, are you going to support my view that the Civil Service is overmanned and feather-bedded or not? Yes or no! Straight answer!'

Could I have put this question any more plainly? I don't think so. This was the reply: 'Minister, if I am pressed for a straight answer I shall say that, as far as we can see, looking at it by and large, taking one thing with another, in terms of the average of departments, then in the last analysis it is probably true to say that, at the end of the day, you would find, in general terms that, not to put too fine a point on it, there really was not very much in it one way or the other.'

While I was still reeling from this, he added, no doubt for further clarification, 'As far as one can see, at this stage.'

I made one last attempt. 'Does that mean yes or no?' I asked, without much hope.

'Yes and no,' he replied helpfully.

'Suppose,' I said, 'suppose you *weren't* asked for a straight answer?'

'Ah,' he said happily, 'then I should play for time, Minister.'

Humphrey's never going to change. I certainly will never change him. Today I got nowhere fast. No, not even fast – I got nowhere, slowly and painfully! The conversation finished with Humphrey suggesting that I take the draft home and study it for the next couple of days, because I might then find that it does indeed say what I want it to say. An idiotic time-wasting suggestion, of course. He's just trying to wear me down.

'And if it doesn't say what I want it to say?' I asked testily.

Sir Humphrey smiled. 'Then we shall be happy to redraft it for you, Minister,' he said.

Back to square one.

January 12

I have thought about yesterday's events very carefully. I do not propose to give this draft back to the Department for any more redrafting. I shall write it myself, and not return it until it is too late for them to change it.

I mentioned this to Bernard, and he thought it was a good idea. I told him in the strictest confidence, and I hope I can trust him. I'm sure I can.

[*Hacker reckoned without the pressures that the Civil Service can apply to its own people. Sir Humphrey enquired about the fourth draft report several times over the next two weeks, and observed that Bernard Woolley was giving evasive answers. Finally, Bernard was invited for a disciplinary drink at Sir Humphrey's Club in Pall Mall. We have found a memo about the meeting among Sir Humphrey's private papers. – Ed.*]

B. W. came for a drink at the Club.

I questioned him about the Department's Report to the Think-Tank.

He said, 'You mean, the Minister's report?', a not-insignificant remark.

In answer to my questions as to why we had not yet had it returned to us, he suggested that I ask the Minister. A most unsatisfactory reply.

I explained that I had chosen to ask him. As he remained stubbornly silent, I observed that he did not seem to be replying.

'Yes and no,' he said. He knows full well that this is one of my favourite replies, and I felt obliged to tick him off for impertinence.

In answer to other questions, B.W. insisted that the Minister is doing his boxes conscientiously, but repeatedly refused to explain the delay over the draft report, merely advising me to enquire of the Minister as he (B.W.) was the Minister's *Private* Secretary.

He appeared to be anxious about his situation, and clearly had been put under some obligation by the Minister to treat some piece of information in strict confidence. I therefore decided to increase his anxiety considerably, to the extent that he would be obliged to find a way of either satisfying both myself and his Minister, and therefore showing that he is worthy to be a flyer [*'High Flyer', means young man destined for the very top of the Service – Ed.*] or of taking one side or the other, thereby revealing an inability to walk a tightrope in a high wind.

I therefore reminded him that he was an employee of the DAA. And, admirable though it is to be loyal to his Minister, an average Minister's tenure is a mere eleven months whereas Bernard's career will, he hopes, last until the age of sixty.

B.W. handled the situation with skill. He opted for asking me a hypothetical question, always a good idea.

He asked me, *if* a purely hypothetical Minister were to be unhappy with a departmental draft of evidence to a committee, and *if* the hypothetical Minister were to be planning to replace it with his own hypothetical draft worked out with his own political advisers at his party HQ, and *if* this Minister was planning to bring in his own draft so close to the final date for evidence that there would be no time to re-draft it, and *if* the hypothetical Private Secretary were to be aware of this hypothetical draft – in confidence – should the hypothetical Private Secretary pass on the information to the Perm. Sec. of the hypothetical Department?

A good question. Naturally, I answered B.W. by saying that no Private Secretary should pass on such information, if given in confidence.

B. W. shows more promise than I thought. [*Appleby Papers 23 /RPY /13c*]

January 23rd

It is now two weeks since I decided to take over the Think-Tank report. My final redraft is going well. Frank and his chaps have been hard at work on it, and I've been burning the midnight oil as well. The situation seems to be infuriating Humphrey, which gives me some considerable pleasure.

Today he again asked me about my redraft of the redraft of the draft. 'What about the evidence to the Central Policy Review Staff?' he said.

'You mean the Think-Tank?' I said playing for time.

'Yes Minister.'

'Why do you want it?' I asked.

'So that we can redraft it.'

'That won't be necessary.'

'I think it will, Minister.'

'Humphrey,' I said firmly, 'drafting is not a Civil Service monopoly.'

'It is a highly specialised skill,' he replied, 'which few people outside the Service can master.'

'Nonsense,' I said. 'Drafts are easy. It's a game anyone can play.'

'Not without getting huffed,' he answered. Actually, he's quite witty, really.

I chuckled at his joke, and changed the subject. But he didn't let me get away with it. 'So can I have the draft back, please?' he persisted.

'Of course,' I said, with a smile. He waited. In vain.

'When, Minister?' he asked, trying to smile back, but definitely through clenched teeth.

'Later,' I said airily.

'But *when*?' he snarled through his smile.

'You always say we mustn't rush things,' I said irritatingly.

He then asked me for a straight answer! The nerve of it! However, as he had started to use my terminology, I answered him in his.

'In due course, Humphrey.' I was really enjoying myself. 'In the fullness of time. At the appropriate juncture. When the moment is ripe. When the requisite procedures have been completed. Nothing precipitate, you understand.'

'Minister,' he said, losing all traces of good humour. 'It is getting urgent.'

He was getting rattled. Great. My tactics were a triumph. 'Urgent?' I said blandly. 'You *are* learning a lot of new words.' I don't think I've ever been quite so rude to anyone in my life. I was having a wonderful time. I must try it more often.

'I hope you will forgive me for saying this,' began Sir Humphrey in his iciest manner, 'but I am beginning to suspect that you are concealing something from me.'

I feigned shock, surprise, puzzlement, ignorance – a whole mass of false emotions. 'Humphrey!' I said in my most deeply shocked voice, 'surely we don't have any secrets from each other?'

'I'm sorry Minister, but sometimes one is forced to consider the possibility that affairs are being conducted in a way which, all things being considered, and making all possible allowances, is, not to put too fine a point on it, perhaps not entirely straightforward.' Sir Humphrey was insulting me in the plainest language he could manage in a crisis. Not entirely straightforward, indeed! Clearly, just as it's against the rules of the House to call anyone a liar, it's against the Whitehall code of conduct too.

So I decided to come clean at last. I told him that I have redrafted the redraft myself, that I'm perfectly happy with it, and that I don't want him to redraft it again.

'But . . .' began Sir Humphrey.

'No buts,' I snapped. 'All I get from the Civil Service is delaying tactics.'

'I wouldn't call Civil Service delays "tactics", Minister,' he replied smoothly. 'That would be to mistake lethargy for strategy.'

I asked him if we hadn't already set up a committee to investigate delays in the Civil Service. He concurred.

'What happened to it?' I asked.

'Oh,' he said, brushing the matter aside, 'it hasn't met yet.'

'Why not?' I wanted to know.

'There . . . seems to have been a delay,' he admitted.

It is vital that I make Humphrey realise that there is a real desire for radical reform in the air. I reminded him that the All-Party Select Committee on Administrative Affairs, which I founded, has been a great success.

This was probably an error, because he immediately asked me what it has achieved. I was forced to admit that it hasn't actually achieved anything *yet*, but I pointed out that the party is very pleased by it.

'Really?' he asked. 'Why?'

'Ten column inches in the *Daily Mail* last Monday, for a start,' I replied proudly.

'I see,' he said coldly, 'the government is to measure its success in column inches, is it?'

'Yes . . . and no,' I said with a smile.

But he was deeply concerned about my redraft of the draft report.

108

'Minister,' he said firmly, 'the evidence that you are proposing to submit is not only untrue, it is – which is much more serious – unwise.' One of Humphrey's most telling remarks so far, I think. 'We have been through this before: *the expanding Civil Service is the result of parliamentary legislation, not bureaucratic empire building.*'

I begin to think that Sir Humphrey really believes this.

'So,' I said, 'when this comes up at Question Time you want me to tell Parliament it's their fault that the Civil Service is so big?'

'It's the truth, Minister,' he insisted.

He can't seem to grasp that I don't want the truth, I want something I can tell Parliament.

I spelled it out to him. 'Humphrey, you are my Permanent Secretary. Are you going to support me?'

'We shall always support you as your standard-bearer, Minister – but not as your pall-bearer.'

There seemed to be a vaguely threatening air about these remarks. I demanded to know what he was actually *saying*. As I was becoming more and more heated, he was becoming icier and icier.

'I should have thought,' he pronounced, in his most brittle voice with excessive clarity of enunciation, somewhat reminiscent of Dame Edith Evans as Lady Bracknell, 'that my meaning was crystal clear. Do not give such a report to a body whose recommendations are to be published.'

As always, he has completely missed the point. I explained that it is *because* the report is to be published that I am submitting the evidence. *I*, the Minister, am to be the judge of when to keep secrets, *not* the permanent officials.

I appeared to have silenced him completely. Then, after a rather long pause for thought, he enquired if he might make one more suggestion.

'Only if it's in plain English,' I replied.

'If you must do this damn silly thing,' he said, 'Don't do it in this damn silly way.'

January 24th

On the way to Number Ten this morning Bernard showed me the agenda for Cabinet. To my horror, I was informed that Cabinet was due to discuss my proposal to close down the Land Registry – or what was *described* as my proposal! I'd never heard of it till that moment. It is a scheme to transfer residual functions to the Property Services Agency. The idea is to reduce the number of autonomous government departments, in which there has been a 9¾% rise. Bernard told me I'd initialled it. God knows when – I suppose it must have been in a red box sometime over the last few weeks but I don't recall it. I've been working on the Think-Tank report and nothing else for the last week or more. Anyway, I can't remember every paper I struggle through at one or two a.m. – in fact, I can hardly remember any of them. There has to be a better system than this.

Bernard assured me that I didn't really need to know much about the proposal because his information on the grapevine, through the Private Office network, was that the proposal would go through on the nod.

[*Regrettably, this situation was not as uncommon as the reader might suppose. Because of both the pressure of time and the complexity of much legislation, Ministers frequently had to propose measures to Cabinet that they themselves either had not read or did not fully understand. Hence the distinction sometimes drawn between Minister- ial policy, i.e. policies about which the Minister has strong personal views or commitments, and Ministry policy, i.e. most policy – Ed.*]

January 25th
Today was the blackest day so far. Perhaps not only the blackest day since I became a Minister, but the blackest day since I went into politics.

I am deeply depressed.

However, I feel I must record the events of the day, and I'll do so in the order in which they occurred.

It appears that Sir Humphrey went to the usual weekly Permanent Secretaries meeting this morning. It seems that he was ticked off by a couple of his colleagues when he revealed that I had written the draft report for the Think-Tank.

Humphrey complained to Bernard about my behaviour, it seems, and Bernard – who seems to be the only one I can totally trust – told me. Apparently Sir Frederick Stewart (Perm. Sec. of the FCO) actually said to Humphrey that once you allow a Minister to write a draft report, the next thing you know they'll be dictating policy.

Incredible!

It is true, of course. I have learned that he who drafts the document wins the day.

[*This is the reason why it was common Civil Service practice at this time to write the Minutes of a meeting* BEFORE *the meeting took place. This achieves two things. First, it helps the chairman or secretary to*

110

ensure that the discussion follows the lines agreed beforehand and that the right points are made by somebody. And second, as busy men generally cannot quite remember what was agreed at meetings, it is extremely useful and convenient to lay it down in advance. Only if the conclusions reached at a meeting are radically different or diametrically opposed to what has been previously written in the minutes will the officials have to re-write them. Thus it is that pre-written minutes can dictate the results of many meetings, regardless of what may be said or agreed by those actually present. – Ed.]

Sir Humphrey and Sir Frederick were discussing Humphrey's plan (*not* mine, I may add!) for reducing the number of autonomous government departments, when they encountered Dr Donald Hughes,[1] who overheard their conversation.

Hughes revealed that the Think-Tank recommendation accepted the idea of reducing the number of autonomous government departments. This news came as a profound shock to Sir Humphrey, because not all the Ministerial evidence has been taken – ours, for instance!

However, it seems that they have reported unofficially, and clearly the report is not going to change now, no matter what we say. Dr Hughes explained cynically to Sir Humphrey that the Central Policy Review Staff do not sully their elevated minds with anything as squalid as evidence from Ministers!

Sir Humphrey, at first, was not unhappy with Donald Hughes's news. Naturally, as an experienced civil servant, a proposal to reduce and simplify the administration of government conjured up in Humphrey's mind a picture of a large intake of new staff specifically to deal with the reductions.

However, this is not the plan at all. Humphrey informed me, at an urgently convened meeting at nine a.m. this morning [*Tautology – Ed.*] that Dr Donald Hughes had made these points:

1 That Jim Hacker is always seeking to reduce overmanning in the Civil Service.
2 That he is going to succeed, at last.
3 And that to facilitate this matter, the Treasury, the Home Office and the Civil Service Department have all proposed abolishing the Department of Administrative Affairs.
4 And that 'the PM is smiling on the plan' (his very words).

[1] Dr Donald Hughes was the Prime Minister's Senior Policy Adviser, brought into government from outside. Tough, intelligent, hard-bitten and with no love for senior civil servants.

Appalling! My job's at stake.

It seems that the PM is entranced by the idea, on the grounds that it is neat, clean, dramatic, and will be politically popular.

The scheme is that all the DAA's functions will be subsumed by other departments.

And my fate? Apparently it is to be presented to the Press and public that I have won through with a public-spirited self-sacrificing policy, and I'm to be kicked upstairs to the Lords.

Donald Hughes, rubbing salt in the wound, apparently described it as 'approbation, elevation and castration, all in one stroke'. It seems he suggested that I should take the title Lord Hacker of Kamikaze.

Apparently Hughes was very pleased with himself, and with this plan, presumably because of his own crusade against Civil Service extravagance, bureaucracy and waste. Ironically, I agree with him on all that – but not at the expense of *my* job, thank you very much.

This certainly confirms my instincts, that some political Cabinet in-fighting was due to start up again, and clearly we have a huge fight on our hands. Everyone's against us. The Perm. Secs. of the Treasury, Home Office and Civil Service Department all stand to gain more power and influence. So do my Cabinet colleagues running those departments. And, of course, I always knew that the DAA was a political graveyard and that the PM might have been handing me a poisoned chalice – after all, I did run Martin's leadership campaign against the PM – whose motto, incidentally, is 'In Defeat, Malice – in Victory, Revenge!'

It seems that Donald Hughes, to do him justice, also pointed out that Humphrey would also be on the way out. 'There's a Job Centre in the Horseferry Road,' he had said maliciously. 'The number 19 stops right outside.'

This is the only remotely amusing thing I've heard in the last twenty-four hours. I shouldn't think Humphrey's been on a bus since he left Oxford.

So when Humphrey brought me up-to-date this morning, I was appalled. I could hardly believe it at first. I told Humphrey I was appalled.

'You're appalled?' he said, 'I'm appalled.'

Bernard said he was appalled, too.

And, there's no doubt about it, the situation is appalling.

I have no doubt that the situation is as described by Sir Humphrey as described by Donald Hughes. It rings true. And Humphrey, yesterday, saw the joint Departmental proposal made by the Treasury,

Home Office and Civil Service Department. And Hughes is very close to the PM too, so he must know what's going on.

I asked Humphrey if I'd get another job, whether or not I was sent to the Lords. Which, incidentally, I shall definitely refuse if it is offered.

'There is a rumour,' replied Sir Humphrey gravely, 'of a new post. Minister with general responsibility for Industrial Harmony.'

This was the worst news yet. Industrial Harmony. That means strikes.[1]

From now on, every strike in Britain will be my fault. Marvellous!

I pondered this for some moments. My reverie was interrupted by Sir Humphrey enquiring in a sepulchral tone: 'Have you considered what might happen to *me*, Minister? I'll probably be sent to Ag. and Fish. The rest of my career dedicated to arguing about the cod quota.'

Bernard dared to smile a little smile, and Humphrey turned on him. 'And as for you, young man, if your Minister bites the dust your reputation as a flyer – such as it is – will be hit for six. You'll probably spend the rest of your career in the Vehicle Licensing Centre in Swansea.'

'My God,' said Bernard.

We sat in silence, lost in our own tragic thoughts, for some considerable time. I heaved a sigh. So did Humphrey. Then Bernard.

Of course, the whole thing is Sir Humphrey's fault. Reducing the number of autonomous government departments? An idiotic proposal, playing right into the hands of our enemies. I said so. He replied that it's all my fault, because of my proposal to the Think-Tank to carry out the phased reduction of the Civil Service.

I pooh-poohed this as a ridiculous suggestion because the Think-Tank hasn't even *seen* our report yet. But Humphrey revealed that the Party sent an advance copy to the PM from Central House.

So perhaps we've both dropped ourselves in it. Anyway, there was no point in arguing about it, and I asked Humphrey for suggestions.

There was another gloomy silence.

'We could put a paper up,' he said finally.

'Up what?' I asked. Brilliant!

Humphrey asked me if *I* had any suggestions. I hadn't. We turned to Bernard.

'What do you think, Bernard?'

[1] Hacker was clearly right about this. On the same euphemistic principle, the Ministry of War was renamed the Ministry of Defence, and the Department responsible for unemployment was called the Department of Employment.

'I think its appalling,' he said. A lot of use he is.

Then Humphrey proposed that we work together on this. This was a novel suggestion, to say the least. I thought his job was to work with me on all occasions. This seemed like an admission. Furthermore, his idea of our working together is generally that he tells me what to do, and I then do it. And look where it's got us!

However, I asked him what he had to suggest.

'With respect, Minister,' he began. This was too much. I told him not to use that insulting language to me ever again! Clearly he was about to reply that anything I had to say on the subject would be beneath contempt.

But Humphrey reiterated that he *really* meant that we should work together. 'I need you,' he said.

I must admit I was rather touched.

Then, to my utter astonishment, he suggested that we sent for Frank Weisel.

Humphrey is clearly a reformed man. Even though it's probably too late to matter!

'You see, Minister, if the Prime Minister is behind a scheme, Whitehall on its own cannot block it. Cabinet Ministers' schemes are easily blocked . . .' he corrected himself at once, '. . . redrafted, but the PM is another matter.'

In a nutshell, his scheme is to fight this plan in Westminster as well as Whitehall. Therefore he believes that Frank can help to mobilise the backbenchers on my behalf.

I suggested that Fleet Street might be of use, if Frank can get the Press on our side. Humphrey blanched and swallowed, but to his credit agreed. 'If there is no other way, even Fleet Street . . .' he murmured.

January 26th

Frank was away yesterday. So we had the meeting with him today.

He'd just heard the news. We asked for his reaction. For the first time that I can remember, he was speechless. He just sat and shook his head sadly. I asked him what suggestions he had.

'I can't think of anything . . . I'm appalled,' he replied.

We all agreed that it was appalling.

So I took charge. 'We've got to stop flapping about like wet hens. We've got to do something to save the Department from closure. Frank, get through to the Whips' office to mobilise the backbenchers and Central House, to stop this before it starts.'

'I'm awfully sorry to quibble again, Minister, but you can't actually stop things before they start,' intervened Bernard, the wet-hen-in-chief. He's really useless in a crisis.

Frank pointed out that this idea of mine wasn't much good, as the scheme would probably be popular with backbenchers. So I pointed out that it was Humphrey's idea, anyway.

Bernard's overnight deliberations led him to propose a publicity campaign in the Press, full page ads praising the Department. He offered us some slogans: ADMINISTRATION SAVES THE NATION and RED TAPE IS FUN.

We just boggled at these ideas. So he then suggested RED TAPE HOLDS THE NATION TOGETHER.

Sometimes I really despair of Bernard.

There was a long pause, after which Humphrey remarked bleakly, 'There's no doubt about it, the writing's on the wall.'

None of us can see any real hope of averting catastrophe.

It's appalling!

January 27th

Life must go on, even while the Sword of Damocles hangs over us.

Today we had a meeting about the Europass. This was a completely new development. I've never even heard of it. Apparently there's been information about it in my boxes for the last couple of nights, but I've been too depressed and preoccupied to grasp anything I've read.

It seems that the Europass is a new European Identity Card, to be carried by all citizens of the EEC. The FCO, according to Humphrey, is willing to go along with the idea as a *quid pro quo* for a settlement over the butter mountain, the wine lake, the milk ocean, the lamb war, and the cod stink.

Apparently the PM wants me to introduce the necessary legislation.

I'm *horrified* by this.

Sir Humphrey was surprised at my reaction. He'd thought it was a good idea as I'm known to be pro-Europe, and he thinks that a Europass will simplify administration in the long run.

Frank and I tried to explain to the officials that for me to introduce such a scheme would be political suicide. The British people do not want to carry compulsory identification papers. I'll be accused of trying to bring in a police state, when I'm still not fully recovered from the fuss about the Data Base. 'Is this what we fought two world wars

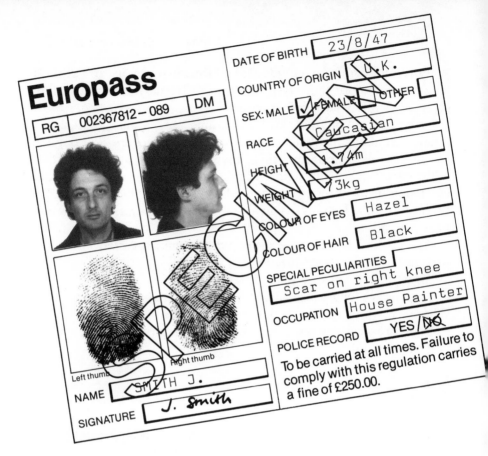

Europass

RG 002367812 – 089 DM

DATE OF BIRTH 23/8/47
COUNTRY OF ORIGIN U.K.
SEX: MALE ✓ FEMALE OTHER
RACE Caucasian
HEIGHT 1.74m
WEIGHT 73kg
COLOUR OF EYES Hazel
COLOUR OF HAIR Black
SPECIAL PECULIARITIES Scar on right knee
OCCUPATION House Painter
POLICE RECORD YES / NO

To be carried at all times. Failure to comply with this regulation carries a fine of £250.00.

Left thumb   Right thumb

NAME SMITH J.
SIGNATURE J. Smith

for?' I can hear the backbenchers cry.

'But it's nothing more than a sort of driving licence,' said Humphrey.

'It's the last nail in my coffin,' said I.

'You might get away with calling it the Euroclub Express,' said Bernard. I told him to shut up or get out.

Frank asked why we had to introduce it, not the FCO? A good question.

'I understand,' explained Humphrey, 'that the PM did originally suggest that the FCO introduce the measure, but the Secretary of State for Foreign and Commonwealth Affairs suggested that it was a Home Office measure, and then the Home Office took the view that it is essentially an administrative matter. The PM agreed.'

Frank said, 'They're all playing pass the parcel.'

Can you blame them, when they can hear it ticking?

Humphrey then observed mournfully that the identity card bill would probably be the last action of our Department.

Frank and I, unlike the civil servants, were still puzzled that such a

116

proposal as the Europass could even be seriously under consideration by the FCO. We can both see clearly that it is wonderful ammunition for the anti-Europeans. I asked Humphrey if the Foreign Office doesn't realise how damaging this would be to the European ideal?

'I'm sure they do, Minister,' he said. 'That's why they support it.'

This was even more puzzling, since I'd always been under the impression that the FO is pro-Europe. 'Is it or isn't it?' I asked Humphrey.

'Yes and no,' he replied of course, 'if you'll pardon the expression. The Foreign Office is pro-Europe because it is really anti-Europe. In fact the Civil Service was united in its desire to make sure the Common Market didn't work. That's why we went into it.'

This sounded like a riddle to me. I asked him to explain further. And basically, his argument was as follows: Britain has had the same foreign policy objective for at least the last five hundred years – to create a disunited Europe. In that cause we have fought with the Dutch against the Spanish, with the Germans against the French, with the French and Italians against the Germans, and with the French against the Italians and Germans. [*The Dutch rebellion against Philip II of Spain, the Napoleonic Wars, the First World War, and the Second World War – Ed.*]

In other words, divide and rule. And the Foreign Office can see no reason to change when it has worked so well until now.

I was aware of all this, naturally, but I regarded it as ancient history. Humphrey thinks that it is, in fact, current policy. It was necessary for us to break up the EEC, he explained, so we had to get inside. We had previously tried to break it up from the outside, but that didn't work. [*A reference to our futile and short-lived involvement in EFTA, the European Free Trade Association, founded in 1960 and which the UK left in 1972 – Ed.*] Now that we're in, we are able to make a complete pig's breakfast out of it. We have now set the Germans against the French, the French against the Italians, the Italians against the Dutch. . .and the Foreign Office is terribly happy. It's just like old times.

I was staggered by all of this. I thought that all of us who are publicly pro-Europe believed in the European ideal. I said this to Sir Humphrey, and he simply chuckled.

So I asked him: if we don't believe in the European ideal, why are we pushing to increase the membership?

'Same reason,' came the reply. 'It's just like the United Nations. The more members it has, the more arguments you can stir up, and the more futile and impotent it becomes.'

This all strikes me as the most appalling cynicism, and I said so.

Sir Humphrey agreed complacently. 'Yes Minister. We call it diplomacy. It's what made Britain great, you know.'

Frank, like the terrier that he is, wanted to continue worrying away at the problem of the Europass. 'How will the other EEC countries feel about having to carry identity papers? Won't they resist too?'

Sir Humphrey felt not. 'The Germans will love it, the French will ignore it, and the Italians and Irish will be too chaotic to enforce it. Only the British will resent it.' He's right of course.

I must say that, to me, it's all beginning to look suspiciously like a plot to get rid of me. Frank doesn't subscribe to a conspiracy theory on this occasion, on the grounds that I'm to be got rid of *anyway* as my department is to be abolished.

But I've got a sneaking suspicion that the PM just wants to make absolutely sure. Frank told me not to be paranoid, but I think he'd be paranoid if everyone were plotting against him.

'We're on your side, Minister,' Sir Humphrey was trying to be comforting. Life is full of surprises.

Then I had an idea. I suddenly realised that Martin will be on my side. I can't imagine why I didn't think of it before. He's Foreign Secretary – and, to my certain knowledge, Martin is genuinely pro-Europe. (Humphrey calls him 'naïve'). Also I ran his campaign against the PM, and he only stands to lose if I'm squeezed out.

We've arranged a meeting with him tomorrow, at the House. I can't think *how* he can help, exactly, but between us we may find some lever.

January 28th
All is well. The battle is won. My career, Humphrey's career, and the DAA have all been saved by a brilliant piece of political opportunism, of which I am extremely proud. Plus a little bit of luck, of course, But it's been a very satisfactory day.

We all gathered conspiratorially at Martin's office. He was full of his usual second-rate witticisms.

'You've done a Samson act, Jim.'

I, presumably, looked blank.

'You see, you wanted to reduce the Civil Service, and you've done it. You've pulled the whole superstructure down – and buried yourself.'

I didn't know whether I was supposed to smile, or congratulate him on his perception, or what.

Sir Humphrey, of course, couldn't wait to join the analogy game. 'A Pyrrhic victory,' he intoned mournfully, presumably to remind us all that he is a classicist.

I got straight to the point. 'Any ideas?' I asked Martin.

He had none. So we all had another of our tremendous gloomy silences.

Then Frank, fortuitously as it turned out, continued worrying away at the puzzle of why the PM wanted to introduce a Europass. 'I don't understand it. It doesn't make sense. Why can't the PM see the damage it's going to do to the government?'

I agreed, and remarked that this Europass thing is the worst disaster to befall the government since I was made a member of the Cabinet. [*We don't think that Hacker actually meant what he seems to be saying here. – Ed.*]

Martin was quite calm about the Europass. 'Everyone knows it won't happen,' he said.

Who does he mean by 'everyone'? I certainly didn't know it wouldn't happen – but then, I didn't even know it *would* happen till yesterday.

'The PM,' continued Martin, 'has to play along with it till after the Napoleon Prize is awarded.'

Apparently the Napoleon Prize is a NATO award, given once every five years. A gold medal, big ceremony in Brussels, and £100,000. The PM is the front runner. It's awarded to the statesman who has made the biggest contribution to European unity since Napoleon. [*That's if you don't count Hitler – Ed.*]

'The award committee meets in six weeks,' said Martin, 'and so obviously the PM doesn't want to rock the boat until it's in the bag.'

I think I caught Bernard mumbling to himself that you don't put boats in bags, but it was very quiet, I might have misheard, and he refused to repeat what he'd said which makes me think I didn't mishear at all.

'And,' said Martin, reaching the point at last, 'once the prize is won, the PM will obviously dump the Europass.'

I had this wonderful idea. I couldn't quite articulate it. It was slowly forming in the back of my mind. But first I needed some answers.

'Martin,' I asked. 'How many people know about the winner of the Napoleon Prize?'

'It's top secret,' he said. Naturally, I was disappointed. Top secret means that everyone knows.

119

But not this time, apparently. *'Top secret*, top secret,' said Martin.

I was now so excited that I was becoming incoherent. 'Don't you see?' I said. 'Backbenchers . . . leaks . . .'

A puzzled Humphrey asked me if I were referring to the Welsh Nationalist Party.

And at that moment God was on my side. The door opened, and in stepped Dr Donald Hughes. He apologised, and said he'd return later, but I stopped him. I told him that he was the very man I wanted to see, that I wanted his advice, and invited him to take a pew.

He pretended that he was eager to help me. But he warned that if it were a case of shutting stable doors after horses have bolted, even he would be powerless to help.

I said, flatteringly, that I'm sure that he would not be powerless. I put it to him that I was in a serious moral dilemma – which, of course, I invented at that very moment.

My dilemma was this, I said. I told Hughes that I knew that a backbencher was planning to table a question to the PM about whether or not the Europass is to be adopted by Britain.

Hughes was immediately jumpy. 'Which backbencher? The Europass is top secret.'

'Like the winner of the Napoleon Prize?' I asked.

We eyed each other carefully – I wasn't entirely sure of my next move, but thankfully Bernard stepped in with an inspirational reply. 'I think the Minister means a hypothetical backbencher,' he said. Good old Bernard.

Hughes said that it was highly improbable.

I ignored that, and explained that if the question were to be asked, there were only two possible replies: if the PM says *yes* it would be damaging to the government in the country – but if the PM says *no* it would be even more damaging to the government in Europe. And to the PM personally – in view of the Napoleon Prize.

Hughes nodded, and waited. So I continued. 'Suppose a hypothetical Minister got wind of this hypothetical backbencher's question, in advance, what should he do?'

'The only responsible course for a loyal minister,' he said carefully, 'would be to see that the question was not tabled. That must be obvious.'

'It's a serious business trying to suppress an MP's question,' I said. Of course, he and I both knew that, as yet, there was no question and no such backbencher – but that there could be, if I chose to set it up.

'The only way to stop him,' I offered, 'might be to let the backbencher table a question asking the PM to squash rumours about the closure of the Department of Administrative Affairs.'

There it was. My offer of a deal. Out in the open. Hughes paused to consider, just for a few moments, in case he could see a way out. But there was none.

And, to his credit, he handled it superbly. At once out came all the appropriate phrases: 'But I'm sure . . . whatever made you think? . . . no question of anything but the fullest support . . .' etc.

Then Humphrey, who'd got the idea at last, moved in for the kill. 'But you said only a few days ago that the plan to abolish the Department had been put up and the PM was smiling on it.'

'Smiling *at* it,' said Donald Hughes smoothly. 'Smiling *at* it, not *on* it. The idea was ridiculous, laughable, out of the question. A joke.' Beautifully done – I take my hat off to him.

So I asked him for a Minute from the PM's office, to be circulated to all departments within twenty-four hours, scotching the rumour. So that we could all share the joke.

'Do you really think it's necessary?' he asked.

'Yes,' replied Humphrey, Bernard, Frank, Martin and I. In unison.

Hughes said that in that case, he was sure it could be arranged, that it would be a pleasure, how much he'd enjoyed chatting to us all, excused himself and left. Presumably he hurried straight to Number Ten.

Game, set and match. One of my most brilliant performances. I am exceedingly pleased with myself.

Bernard asked, after Donald Hughes had gone, if Hughes can really fix it for us. 'Don't Prime Ministers have a mind of their own?' he asked.

'Certainly,' I said to Bernard. 'But in the words of Chuck Colson, President Nixon's henchman, when you've got them by the balls, their hearts and minds will follow.'

6

The Right to Know

February 1st
Today I had an environmental issue to deal with. A deputation of several environmentalists brought me a petition. Six fat exercise books, full of signatures. There must be thousands of signatures, if not hundreds of thousands.

They were protesting about my proposed new legislation to sort out all the existing confusions and anomalies in the present system – not that you can *call* it a system – which is a mess, a hotchpotch. Local authorities, tourist authorities, national parks, the National Trust, the Countryside Commission, the CPRE[1] are all backbiting and buckpassing and nobody knows where they are and nothing gets done. The sole purpose of the new legislation is to tidy all this up and make all these wretched committees work together.

I explained this to the deputation. 'You know what committees are?' I said. 'Always squabbling and procrastinating and wasting everyone's time.'

'*We* are a committee,' said one of them, an unprepossessing bespectacled female of indeterminate age but clear upper-middle-class Hampstead origins. She seemed rather offended.

I explained that I didn't mean *her* sort of committee; all that I was trying to do was create a new authority with clear simple procedures. Public money will be saved. It seems to me that it should be welcome to everyone.

However, these representatives of the Hampstead middle-class were worried about some place called Hayward's Spinney. Apparently it is going to lose its protected status under the new scheme – like one or two other places – it's simply not economic to administer it properly.

[1] The Council for the Preservation of Rural England.

122

But it seems that Hayward's Spinney is regarded by some of these cranks as a vital part of Britain's heritage. 'The badgers have dwelt in it for generations,' spluttered an elderly upper-class socialist of the Michael Foot patrician ilk.

'How do you know?' I asked, simply out of curiosity.

'It said so in *The Guardian*,' said an intense young man in hobnail boots.

Some reason for believing anything! You've only got to be in public life for about a week before you start to question if the newspapers are even giving you today's date with any accuracy! However, the young man thrust a copy of *The Guardian* at me.

I looked at the story he had circled in red. Actually, what *The Guardian* said was: 'The bodgers have dwelt in it for in it for generators.'

I read it aloud, and laughed, but they appeared to have absolutely no sense of humour. Then the middle-aged lady in a brown tweed skirt that enveloped mighty hips demanded, 'How would you feel if you were going to have office blocks built all over your garden by a lot of giant badgers?'

Giant badgers? I tried not to laugh at this Monty Pythonesque vision, while another of these freaks continued self-righteously, 'There's nothing special about man, Mr Hacker. We're not above nature. We're all a part of it. Men are animals too, you know.'

Obviously I knew that already. I'd just come from the House of Commons.

Bernard helped me get rid of them after about ten minutes. I made no promises to them, and gave them the usual bromides about all views being taken into consideration at the appropriate stage. But I am concerned that no one in the Department warned me that unifying the administration of the countryside would mean removing special protected status from these blasted badgers. Not that I give a damn about badgers, but I have been allowed to tell Parliament and the Press that no loss of amenity was involved.

I should take this matter up with Humphrey tomorrow.

I shall also take up the matter of why my time is being wasted with footling meetings of this kind, when I want to spend much more time meeting junior staff here, getting to know their problems, and generally finding out how to run the Department more efficiently.

[*We discovered a remarkable exchange of memos between Sir Humphrey Appleby and Bernard Woolley, written during this week.* – *Ed.*]

DEPARTMENT OF
ADMINISTRATIVE AFFAIRS

From the Permanent Under–Secretary of State

B.W. ———

I gather that the Minister has been arranging for himself unsupervised meetings with junior members of the Department — Assistant Secretaries, Principals, and even right down to Higher Executive Officers. Please explain

J.A.   1/ii

DEPARTMENT OF
ADMINISTRATIVE AFFAIRS

From the Private Secretary

Sir Humphrey

The Minister wishes to
get to know members
of the Department at
all levels, and to under-
stand what they do and
why. B.W. Feb 1st

DEPARTMENT OF
ADMINISTRATIVE AFFAIRS

From the Permanent Under-Secretary of State

B. W. ——

These meetings must be stopped at once. If the Minister talks to underlings he may learn things that we don't know ourselves. Our whole position could be undermined.

H.A.

2/ii

**DEPARTMENT OF
ADMINISTRATIVE AFFAIRS**

From the Private Secretary

Sir Humphrey

The Minister feels that
such meetings increase
our knowledge. He also
has expressed a wish to
run the Department
better, as things are
now going pretty well.

B.W. Feb. 2nd

DEPARTMENT OF
ADMINISTRATIVE AFFAIRS

From the Permanent Under–Secretary of State

B.W. ——

I think you ought to be very careful. I am puzzled by your recent memos and am wondering if the Minister is being entirely straightforward. I am bound to say that you should give urgent and active consideration to this matter, and ask yourself if you have considered all the implications. Ministerial activities in this area are liable to have consequences which could be unfortunate, or even regrettable.

3/ii

[*Translation: 'Considered all the implications' means 'You are making a complete balls-up of your job.' 'Consequences which could be unfortunate, or even regrettable' means 'You are in imminent danger of being transferred to the War Graves Commission' – Ed.*]

**DEPARTMENT OF
ADMINISTRATIVE AFFAIRS**

From the Private Secretary

Sir Humphrey

I should be grateful
for further advice
on this matter.
B.W. Feb 3rd

DEPARTMENT OF
ADMINISTRATIVE AFFAIRS

From the Permanent Under–Secretary of State

B.W. ——— Please note the following points :

1. You refer to increased knowledge. Desirable and worthy though this ambition is, please remember that it is folly to increase your knowledge at the expense of your authority.

2. When a Minister actually starts to run his Department, things are not going pretty well. They are going pretty badly. It is not the Minister's job to run the Department. It is my job, for which I have had twenty-five years' training and practice.

3. If the Minister were allowed to run the Department we should have:
   (i) chaos
   (ii) innovations
   (iii) public debate
   (iv) outside scrutiny.

4. A Minister has three functions:
   (i) He is an Advocate. He makes the Departments' actions seem plausible to Parliament and the public.
   (ii) He is Our Man in Westminster, steering our legislation through parliament. (N.B. Ours, not his.)
   (iii) He is our Breadwinner. His duty is to fight in Cabinet for the money we need to do our job.

PLEASE NOTE: It's not his function to review departmental procedures and practices with Principals and Higher Executive Officers.

ƒƒA. 4/ii

SIR BERNARD WOOLLEY RECALLS:[1]

Being rather young and green at this time, I was still somewhat puzzled about how to put Sir Humphrey's advice into practice, as the Minister made these diary appointments for himself and was getting thoroughly on top of his work.

I sought a meeting with Sir Humphrey, and began it by attempting to explain that I couldn't prevent the Minister from doing what he wanted if he had the time.

Sir Humphrey was thunderously angry! He asked me why the Minister had free time. He told me to ensure that the Minister never had free time, and that it was my fault if he had. My job was to create activity. The Minister must make speeches, go on provincial visits, foreign junkets, meet deputations, work through mountains of red boxes, and be forced to deal with crises, emergencies and panics.

If the Minister made spaces in his diary, I was to fill them up again. And I was to make sure that he spent his time where he was not under our feet and would do no damage – the House of Commons for instance.

However, I do recall that I managed to redeem myself a little when I was able to inform Sir Humphrey that the Minister was – even as we spoke – involved in a completely trivial meeting about preserving badgers in Warwickshire.

In fact, he was so pleased that I suggested that I should try to find some other threatened species with which to involve the Minister. Sir Humphrey replied that I need not look far – Private Secretaries who could not occupy their Ministers were a threatened species.

February 2nd

This morning I raised the matter of the threatened furry animals, and the fact that I told the House that no loss of amenity was involved.

Sir Humphrey said that I'd told the House no such thing. The speech had contained the words: 'No *significant* loss of amenity.'

I thought this was the same thing, but Sir Humphrey disabused me. 'On the contrary, there's all the difference in the world, Minister. Almost anything can be attacked as a loss of amenity and almost anything can be defended as not a significant loss of amenity. One must appreciate the significance of *significant*.'

I remarked that six books full of signatures could hardly be called insignificant. Humphrey suggested I look inside them. I did, and to my utter astonishment I saw that there were a handful of signatures in each book, about a hundred altogether at the most. A very cunning ploy – a Press photo of a petition of six fat books is so much more

[1] In conversation with the Editors.

impressive than a list of names on a sheet of Basildon Bond.

And indeed, the publicity about these badgers could really be rather damaging.

However, Humphrey had organised a Press Release which says that the relevant spinney is merely de-registered, not threatened; that badgers are very plentiful all over Warwickshire; that there is a connection between badgers and brucellosis; and which reiterates that there is no 'significant loss of amenity'.

We called in the Press Officer, who agreed with Humphrey that it was unlikely to make the national Press except a few lines perhaps on an inside page of *The Guardian*. The consensus at our meeting was that it is only the urban intellectual middle-class who worry about the preservation of the countryside because they don't have to live in it. They just read about it. Bernard says their protest is rooted more in Thoreau than in anger. I am beginning to get a little tired of his puns.

So we'd dealt satisfactorily with the problems of the animal kingdom. Now I went on to raise the important fundamental question: Why was I not told the full facts before I made the announcement to the House?

Humphrey's reason was astonishing. 'Minister,' he said blandly, 'there are those who have argued – and indeed very cogently – that on occasion there are some things it is better for the Minister not to know.'

I could hardly believe my ears. But there was more to come.

'Minister,' he continued unctuously, 'your answers in the House and at the Press Conference were superb. You were convinced, and therefore convincing. Could you have spoken with the same authority if the ecological pressure group had been badgering you?'

Leaving aside this awful pun, which in any case I suspect might have been unintentional, despite Humphrey's pretensions to wit, I was profoundly shocked by this open assertion of his right to keep me, the people's representative, in ignorance. Absolutely monstrous. I told him so.

He tried to tell me that it is in my best interests, a specious argument if ever I heard one. I told him that it was intolerable, and must not occur again.

And I intend to see that it doesn't.

February 10th

For the past week Frank Weisel and I have been hard at work on a plan to reorganise the Department. One of the purposes was to have assorted officials at all levels reporting to me.

Today I attempted to explain the new system to Sir Humphrey, who effectively refused to listen.

Instead, he interrupted as I began, and told me that he had something to say to me that I might not like to hear. He said it as if this were something new!

As it happens, I'd left my dictaphone running, and his remarks were recorded for posterity. What he actually said to me was: 'Minister, the traditional allocation of executive responsibilities has always been so determined as to liberate the Ministerial incumbent from the administrative minutiae by devolving the managerial functions to those whose experience and qualifications have better formed them for the performance of such humble offices, thereby releasing their political overlords for the more onerous duties and profound deliberations that are the inevitable concomitant of their exalted position.'

I couldn't imagine why he thought I wouldn't want to hear that. It was riveting. Presumably he thought it would upset me – but how can you be upset by something you don't understand a word of?

Yet again, I begged him to express himself in plain English. This request always surprises him, as he is always under the extraordinary impression that he has done so.

Nevertheless, he thought hard for a moment and then, plainly, opted for expressing himself in words of one syllable.

'You are not here to run this Department,' he said.

I was somewhat taken aback. I remarked that I think I am, and the public thinks so too.

'With respect,' he said, and I restrained myself from punching him in the mouth. 'You are wrong and they are wrong.'

He then went on to say that it is *his* job to run the Department. And that my job is to make policy, get legislation enacted and – above all – secure the Department's budget in Cabinet.

'Sometimes I suspect,' I said to him, 'that the budget is all you really care about.'

'It is rather important,' he answered acidly. 'If nobody cares about the budget we could end up with a Department so small that even a Minister could run it.'

I'm sure he's not supposed to speak to me like this.

However, I wasn't upset because I'm sure of my ground. 'Humphrey,' I enquired sternly, 'are we about to have a fundamental disagreement about the nature of democracy?'

As always, he back-pedalled at once when seriously under fire. 'No,

Minister,' he said in his most oily voice, giving his now familiar impression of Uriah Heep, 'we are merely having a demarcation dispute. I am only saying that the menial chore of running a Department is beneath you. You were fashioned for a nobler calling.'

Of course, the soft soap had no effect on me. I insisted on action, now! To that end, we left it that he would look at my reorganisation plan. He promised to do his best to put it into practice, and, to that end, will set up a committee of enquiry with broad terms of reference so that at the end of the day we can take the right decisions based on long-term considerations. He argued that this was preferable to rushing prematurely into precipitate and possibly ill-conceived actions which might have unforeseen repercussions. This seems perfectly satisfactory to me; he has conceded the need for wide-ranging reforms, and we might as well be sure of getting them right.

Meanwhile, while I was quite happy to leave all the routine paperwork to Humphrey and his officials, from now on I was to have direct access to *all* information. Finally, I made it clear that I never again wished to hear the phrase, 'there are some things it is better for a Minister not to know.'

February 12th
Saturday today, and I've been at home in the constituency.

I'm very worried about Lucy. [*Hacker's daughter, eighteen-years-old at this time – Ed.*] She really does seem to be quite unbalanced sometimes. I suppose it's all my fault. I've spent little enough time with her over the years, pressure of work and all that, and it's obviously no coincidence that virtually all my successful colleagues in the House have highly acrimonious relationships with their families and endlessly troublesome adolescent children.

But it can't all be my fault. *Some* of it must be her own fault! Surely!

She was out half the night and came down for a very late breakfast, just as Annie and I were starting an early lunch. She picked up the *Mail* with a gesture of disgust – solely because it's not the *Socialist Worker*, or *Pravda*, I suppose.

I had glanced quickly through all the papers in the morning, as usual, and a headline on a small story on an inside page of *The Guardian* gave me a nasty turn. HACKER THE BADGER BUTCHER. The story was heavily slanted against me and in favour of the sentimental wet liberals – not surprising really, every paper has to pander to its typical reader.

Hacker admitted that removed protected status from Hayward's Spinney could mean the end of the badger colony.

A spokesman for the Society for the Preservation of British Wildlife said: "Hacker has singed the badgers' death warrant."

Good old *Grauniad*.

I nobly refrained from saying to Lucy, 'Good afternoon' when she came down, and from making a crack about a sit-in when she told us she'd been having a lie-in.

However, I *did* ask her why she was so late home last night, to which she replied, rather pompously, 'There are some things it is better for a father not to know.' 'Don't *you* start,' I snapped, which, not surprisingly, puzzled her a little.

She told me she'd been out with the trots. I was momentarily sympathetic and suggested she saw the doctor. Then I realised she meant the Trotskyites. I'd been slow on the uptake because I didn't know she was a Trotskyite. Last time we talked she'd been a Maoist.

'Peter's a Trot,' she explained.

'Peter?' my mind was blank.

'You've only met him about fifteen times,' she said in her most scathing tones, the voice that teenage girls specially reserve for when they speak to their fathers.

Then Annie, who could surely see that I was trying to work my way through five red boxes this weekend, asked me to go shopping with her at the 'Cash and Carry', to unblock the kitchen plug hole, and mow the lawn. When I somewhat irritably explained to her about the boxes, she said they could wait!

'Annie,' I said, 'it may have escaped your notice that I am a Minister of the Crown. A member of Her Majesty's Government. I do a *fairly* important job.'

Annie was strangely unsympathetic. She merely answered that I have twenty-three thousand civil servants to help me, whereas she had none. 'You can play with your memos later,' she said. 'The drains need fixing now.'

I didn't even get round to answering her, as at that moment Lucy stretched across me and spilled marmalade off her knife all over the cabinet minutes. I tried to scrape it off, but merely succeeded in buttering the minutes as well.

I told Lucy to get a cloth, a simple enough request, and was astounded by the outburst that it provoked. 'Get it yourself,' she snarled. 'You're not in Whitehall now, you know. "Yes Minister" . . . "No Minister" . . . "Please may I lick your boots, Minister?"'

I was speechless. Annie intervened on my side, though not as firmly as I would have liked. 'Lucy, darling,' she said in a tone of mild reproof, 'that's not fair. Those civil servants are always kowtowing to Daddy, but they never take any real notice of him.'

This was too much. So I explained to Annie that only two days ago I won a considerable victory at the Department. And to prove it I showed her the pile of five red boxes stuffed full of papers.

She didn't think it proved anything of the sort. 'For a short while you were getting the better of Sir Humphrey Appleby, but now they've snowed you under again.'

I thought she'd missed the point. I explained my reasoning: that Humphrey had said to me, *in so many words*, that there are some things that it's better for a Minister not to know, which means that he hides things from me. Important things, perhaps. So I have now insisted that I'm told *everything* that goes on in the Department.

However, her reply made me rethink my situation. She smiled at me with genuine love and affection, and said:

'Darling, how did you get to be a Cabinet Minister? You're such a clot.'

Again I was speechless.

Annie went on, 'Don't you see, you've played right into his hands? He must be utterly delighted. You've given him an open invitation to swamp you with useless information.'

I suddenly saw it all with new eyes. I dived for the red boxes – they contained feasibility studies, technical reports, past papers of assorted committees, stationery requisitions . . . junk!

It's Catch-22. Those bastards. Either they give you so little information that you don't know the facts, or so much information that you can't *find* them.

You can't win, it seems. They get you coming and going.

February 13th
The contrasts in a Minister's life are supposed by some people to keep you sane and ordinary and feet-on-the-ground. I think they're making me schizoid.

All week I'm protected and cosseted and cocooned. My every wish is somebody's command. (Not on matters of real substance of course, but in little everyday matters.) My letters are written, my phone is answered, my opinion is sought, I'm waited on hand and foot and I'm driven everywhere by chauffeurs, and everyone addresses me with the utmost respect as if I were a kind of God.

But this is all on government business. The moment I revert to party business or private life, the whole apparatus deserts me. If I go to a party meeting, I must get myself there, by bus if necessary; if I go home on constituency business, no secretary accompanies me; if I have a party speech to make, there's no one to type it out for me. So every weekend I have to adjust myself to doing the washing up and unblocking the plug hole after five days of being handled like a priceless cut-glass antique.

And this weekend, although I came home on Friday night on the train, five red boxes arrived on Saturday morning in a chauffeur-driven car!

Today I awoke, having spent a virtually sleepless night pondering over what Annie had said to me. I staggered down for breakfast, only to find – to my amazement – a belligerent Lucy lying in wait for me. She'd found yesterday's *Guardian* and had been reading the story about the badgers.

'There's a story about you here, Daddy,' she said accusingly.

I said I'd read it. Nonetheless she read it out to me. 'Hacker the badger butcher,' she said.

'Daddy's read it, darling,' said Annie, loyally. As if stone deaf, Lucy read the whole story aloud. I told her it was a load of rubbish, she looked disbelieving, so I decided to explain in detail.

'One: I am not a badger butcher. Two: the badger is not an endangered species. Three: the removal of protective status does not necessarily mean the badgers will be killed. Four: if a few badgers have to be sacrificed for the sake of a master plan that will save Britain's natural heritage – tough!'

Master plan is always a bad choice of phrase, particularly to a generation brought up on Second World War films. 'Ze master plan, mein Führer,' cried my darling daughter, giving a Nazi salute. 'Ze end justifies ze means, does it?'

Apart from the sheer absurdity of a supporter of the Loony Left having the nerve to criticise someone *else* for believing that the end justifies the means – which I don't or not necessarily, anyway – she is really making a mountain out of a ridiculous molehill.

'It's because badgers haven't got votes, isn't it?' This penetrating question completely floored me. I couldn't quite grasp what she was on about.

'If badgers had votes you wouldn't be exterminating them. You'd be up there at Hayward's Spinney, shaking paws and kissing cubs. Ingratiating yourself the way you always do. Yuk!'

Clearly I have not succeeded in ingratiating myself with my own daughter.

Annie intervened again. 'Lucy,' she said, rather too gently I thought, 'that's not a very nice thing to say.'

'But it's true, isn't it?' said Lucy.

Annie said: 'Ye-e-es, it's true . . . but well, he's in politics. Daddy *has* to be ingratiating.'

Thanks a lot.

'It's got to be stopped,' said Lucy. Having finished denouncing me, she was now instructing me.

'Too late.' I smiled nastily. 'The decision's been taken, dear.'

'I'm going to stop it, then,' she said.

Silly girl. 'Fine,' I said. 'That should be quite easy. Just get yourself adopted as a candidate, win a general election, serve with distinction on the backbenches, be appointed a Minister and repeal the act. No problem. Of course, the badgers might be getting on a bit by then.'

She flounced out and, thank God, stayed out for the rest of the day.

[*Meanwhile, Bernard Woolley was becoming increasingly uneasy about keeping secrets from the Minister. He was finding it difficult to accustom himself to the idea that civil servants apply the 'need to know' principle that is the basis of all security activities. Finally he sent a memo to Sir Humphrey, asking for a further explanation as to why the Minister should not be allowed to know whatever he wants to know. The reply is printed opposite – Ed.*]

DEPARTMENT OF
ADMINISTRATIVE AFFAIRS

From the Permanent Under–Secretary of State

B.W. -

This country is governed by ministers making decisions from the various
alternative proposals which we offer them.

If they had all the facts, they would see many other possibilities, some
of which would not be in the public interest. Nonetheless, they might
formulate their own plans instead of choosing from the two or three which
we put up.

So long as we formulate the proposals, we can guide them towards a
correct decision.

We in the Service are not foolish or misguided enough to believe that
there is one single correct solution to any problem. However, it is
our public duty to guide the Minister towards what we like to call
"the common ground".

In order to guide the Minister towards the common ground, key words
should be inserted with a proposal to make it attractive:

Ministers will generally accept proposals which contain the words
simple, quick, popular, and cheap.

Ministers will generally throw out proposals which contain the words
complicated, lengthy, expensive and controversial.

Above all, if you wish to describe a proposal in a way that guarantees
that a Minister will reject it, describe it as courageous.

Remember, guiding ministers in this fashion is what has made Britain
what she is today.

AA. 13/ii

139

[*It is worth examining Sir Humphrey Appleby's choice of words in this memo. The phrase 'the common ground', for example, was much used by Sir Antony Part, former Permanent Secretary at the Department of Industry. It seemed to mean policies that the Civil Service can pursue without disturbance whichever Party is in power. 'Courageous' as used in this context is an even more damning word than 'controversial'. 'Controversial' only means 'this will lose you votes'. 'Courageous' means 'this will lose you the election' – Ed.*]

February 14th

Sunday February 13th

Dear Daddy,
Tomorrow, I and my fellow student and lover, Pete, intend to hold a 24 hour protest vigil at Hayward's Spinney in aid of the Badgers.
The Save-The-Badgers vigil will be in the nude, as befits St Valentine's Day.
We shall put the announcement of this event out to the press and media if the badgers' protection is not restored by 5 pm Monday February 14th, or some satisfactory assurance given.
We shall hold a nude press conference at 6 pm.
Lucy Hacker

[*The above letter was found by Bernard Woolley when he opened Hacker's boxes in the office on Monday 14th February. The envelope was addressed to 'Daddy' but rules state that Private Secretaries open every letter of every classification up to and including* TOP SECRET, *unless specifically marked* PERSONAL. *This was a letter not marked*

140

PERSONAL. *Hacker's diary continues. – Ed.*]

This afternoon seemed to last an eternity. I think I've more or less got over the slings and arrows of outrageous fortune, but it was one of the worst afternoons of my political life so far. However, I shall relate it from the start. Firstly, there was Jak's cartoon in the *Standard*.

Then, on my return from Cabinet and Cabinet Committee after lunch, Bernard and Humphrey edged into the office looking extremely anxious. I asked if anything was wrong.

For the next four minutes they appeared to speak in riddles.

'Shall we say, a slight embarrassment,' said Sir Humphrey.

'How slight?' I asked.

First he rambled on about not wishing to overstate the case or suggest that there was any cause for undue alarm, but nevertheless . . . etc. etc. I told him to get on with it, he told me he had a confession to make, and I told him to make a clean breast of it.

'Not the happiest of phrases, in the circumstances,' he replied enigmatically. I still hadn't the foggiest idea what he was talking

141

about, although it was soon to become only too clear.

But Humphrey couldn't find a way to tell me the bad news. Extraordinary. First he said there was to be a twenty-four-hour protest vigil in Hayward's Spinney, conducted by a girl student and her boyfriend. I could see no problem in two irresponsible layabouts trying – and failing – to attract attention to themselves.

And like an idiot, I said so. (If there's one lesson I learned today it is not to shoot from the hip. Wait until you know the full facts before giving *any* response, if you don't want to finish up looking like a proper Charlie.)

But I got an attack of verbal diarrhoea. 'Nobody's interested,' I said. 'Everyone's fed up with these ghastly students. They're just exhibitionists, you know.'

'In this case,' remarked Sir Humphrey, suddenly becoming less enigmatic, 'they seem to have something to exhibit. It is to be a nude protest vigil.'

This did seem to present a problem. It would clearly attract considerable Press interest, and could even get onto the front pages of the tabloids. Regrettably, however, Humphrey hadn't given me the full picture, so I went on and on talking, making myself seem more idiotic every minute. 'Really, I don't know what gets into these students. Appalling. Quite shameless. And it's their parents' fault. Don't bring them up properly, let them run wild and feed them all this trendy middle-class anti-establishment nonsense.' Then I wittered on about the lack of authority nowadays, and how all this student anarchy is a shocking indictment of their parents' lack of discipline.

At this point Humphrey was kind enough to reveal to me that the student's name was Miss Hacker. For a moment I thought it was a coincidence. And then the penny dropped. I've never felt so foolish in my whole life. I'm sure (at least I *think* I'm sure) that Humphrey didn't intend to make any humiliation as complete as possible. But he succeeded. And I'll get him for it one day!

After I picked myself up off the floor, I expressed the hope that the Press might not think it worth going all the way to Warwickshire. Even as I spoke I knew I was talking rubbish – for a story like this the Press would go all the way to the South Pole.

Humphrey and Bernard just looked pityingly at me, and then showed me the letter.

I noted that Lucy was giving out the press release at five p.m. Very professional. Misses the evening papers, which not too many people read, and therefore makes all the dailies. She's learned *something* from being a politician's daughter.

Then Bernard said that he thought he'd better mention that Lucy was ringing up in ten minutes, from a call-box, for an answer.

I asked how we could kill the story. Silence from them both. 'Advise me,' I said.

'What about a bit of parental authority and discipline?' suggested Sir Humphrey. I told him not to be silly.

'If you could make her listen to reason . . .' volunteered Bernard.

I explained to him that she is a sociology student.

'Oh I see,' he said sadly.

Another long pause for thought. Then I suggested calling the police.

Humphrey shook his head, and composed the inevitable headline: MINISTER SETS POLICE ON NUDE DAUGHTER.

'I'm not sure that *completely* kills the story, Minister,' he said.

We sat in one of our tragic silences. Occasional sighs filled the room. Then Humphrey suddenly perked up. 'What if . . .' he said.

'Yes?' I said hopefully.

'What if . . .' he said again, '. . . I looked at the files?'

I'm ashamed to say that I completely lost my temper with him. 'Bloody marvellous!' I shouted. 'Is that what you get over thirty thousand a year for? My daughter's about to get herself all over the front page of the *Sun* and probably page three as well, and all you can think of is the *files!* Brilliant!'

He waited till I finished yelling. 'Nevertheless . . .' he said.

'They're all out there,' said Bernard, quickly indicating the Private Office. Humphrey disappeared as fast as he could, before I could shout at him again.

Bernard and I gazed at each other in despair. 'I wonder what sort of angle they'll take?' I said.

'Wide angle, I should think.' I glared at him. 'Oh, I see what you mean. Sorry.'

All I could think of was the fun the Opposition was going to have with this, next time I had to face questions in the House. 'Does the proud father want to make a statement?' 'Is the Minister's family getting too much exposure?' 'Did the Minister try to conduct a cover-up?' Or even: 'Does the Minister run the Department of Administrative Affairs any better than he runs his family?'

I mentioned the last question to Bernard, because it is my Achilles heel. I added bitterly that I supposed Bernard would want me to tell the world that Sir Humphrey runs the Department.

Bernard seemed genuinely shocked.

'Certainly not, Minister, not I,' he said indignantly. 'I am your Private Secretary.'

'You mean,' I enquired disbelievingly, 'that when the chips are down, you'll be on my side, not Humphrey's?'

Bernard answered very simply: 'Minister, it is my job to see that the chips stay up!'

[*This is, in fact, a precise definition of the Private Secretary's role. – Ed.*]

At that moment Lucy rang in. She was in a call-box. I grabbed the phone. First I tried bluffing. 'I got your little note,' I said, trying to laugh it off. 'You know, for a moment I was taken in. I thought it was serious.' My little laugh sounded false even to me.

'It is serious,' she replied coldly. 'Pete and I are just going to ring the Exchange Telegraph and Press Association, and then we're off to the Spinney.'

Then I grovelled. I begged her to think of the damage to me. She replied that it was the badgers who were going to be exterminated, not I.

She's quite wrong about that! I was about to become the victim of a St Valentine's Day Massacre.

It was clear that she was about to go ahead with her dreadful plan, because I couldn't change my policy on her account, when Humphrey came running through the door waving a file. I've never seen him run before. He was burbling on about a new development and asked if he could speak to Lucy.

He took the phone, opened the file and began to explain his finding. 'I have just come upon the latest report from the Government's Wildlife Inspectors. It throws a new light on the whole issue.'

He went on to explain that, apparently, there is *no* badger colony in Hayward's Spinney. Apparently the wording of the report says: 'The last evidence of badger habitation – droppings, freshly-turned earth, etc. – was recorded eleven years ago.'

Lucy was plainly as astonished as Bernard and I. I was listening in on my other phone. So was Bernard, on his. She asked how come the newspaper had said badgers were there. Humphrey explained that the story about the poor badgers had been leaked to the Press, untruthfully, by a local property developer.

Lucy was immediately willing to believe Humphrey. As far as the Trots are concerned, property developers are Satan's representatives on earth. She asked for the explanation.

144

'The Local Authority have plans to use the Spinney to build a new College of Further Education, but the developer wants to buy it for offices and luxury flats.'

'But,' interrupted Lucy, 'if it's protected, he can't.'

'No,' agreed Sir Humphrey, 'but nor can the Council. And he knows that, if they can't, they'll spend the money on something else. Then, in twelve months, he'll move in, show that there's no badgers after all, get the protection removed and build his offices.'

From the complete silence, I could tell that Lucy was profoundly shocked. Then Humphrey added: 'It's common practice among property developers. Shocking isn't it?'

I had no idea Humphrey felt this way about property developers. I had thought he rather liked them.

Lucy asked Humphrey if there was any wildlife at all in the Spinney.

'Yes, there is some,' said Humphrey, looking through the file. 'It's apparently been used as a rubbish dump by people from Birmingham, so there are lots of rats.'

'Rats,' she said quietly. Lucy hates rats.

'Yes, thousands of them,' said Humphrey and added generously, 'Still, I suppose they're wildlife too, in their way.' He paused and then remarked: 'It would be a pity to play into the developer's hands, wouldn't it?'

'I suppose it would,' she answered. Clearly the Save-the-Badgers vigil was off!

Humphrey added, with great warmth and total hypocrisy: 'But do let me say how much I respect your views and commitment.'

She didn't ask to speak to me again. She just rang off. The crisis was over as suddenly as it had begun. There was no way she was going to conduct a nude love-in with lots of rats in the vicinity – other than the Press, of course.

I congratulated Humphrey profusely. 'It was nothing, Minister,' he said self-effacingly, 'it was all in the files.'

I was amazed by the whole thing. What a cunning bastard that property developer must be. I asked Humphrey to show me the report.

Suddenly he became his old evasive self. He told me it wasn't awfully interesting. Again I asked to see it. He held it behind his back like a guilty schoolboy.

Then I had an extraordinary insight. I asked him if the story were true. He claimed he didn't understand my question. So I asked him, again, clearly, if there had been one word of truth in that amazingly convenient story which he had just told Lucy.

He eyed me, and then enquired slowly and carefully: 'Do you really want me to answer that question, Minister? Don't answer hastily.'

It was a good question. A very good question. I could think of no advantage in knowing the truth, if my suspicions were correct. And a huge disadvantage – I would be obliged to be dishonest with Lucy, something I have never done and will never do!

'No,' I said after a few moments, 'um, Humphrey, don't bother to answer.'

'Quite so,' he said, as smug as I've ever seen him. 'Perhaps you would care to note that there *are* some things that it is better for a Minister not to know.'

7

Jobs for
the Boys

[*In the middle of February Jim Hacker came within a hair's-breadth of
involving himself in a scandal that would have rocked the government
and brought an ignominious and premature end to his political career.
Ironically Hacker would have found himself taking responsibility for
events with which he had no real connection or involvement – but for
which as Minister, he would have been answerable. – Ed.*]

February 21st

I arrived at the office in a rather good mood today. I'd done all my
boxes. I was feeling thoroughly on top of the job. I'd handled all my
PQ's [*Parliamentary Questions – Ed.*] rather well yesterday, given a
good speech last night at a dinner, and was looking forward to a
broadcast that I'm due to make tomorrow. All splendid publicity. I
find that people are at last beginning to know who I am, as a result of
the high profile I've been managing recently.

I asked Bernard what the broadcast discussion would be about.
NATO, I thought. Bernard said that, in fact, it would be about
co-partnership in industry.

I knew it was something like that. Some sort of partnership, at any
rate.

The discussion would contain the usual compulsory BBC ingre-
dients – one politician, one employer and one trades unionist.

I noticed that the trades unionist in question was Joe Morgan, who
had been the TUC representative on the Solihull project. I remarked
that this was good, because it meant we could talk about the project
on the air.

To my surprise, this rather non-controversial remark was greeted
with much anxiety by Sir Humphrey.

'Minister, you're not proposing to refer to the Solihull project on
the air?'

'I certainly am,' I said. 'It's a shining example of a successful collaboration between government and private industry.'

'Why do you say that?' he asked.

For a moment, I couldn't think why. Then I remembered. 'Because you said it was,' I pointed out. 'Why? Have you changed your mind?'

'No,' he said carefully, 'but . . . I would be much happier if you omitted such references from the broadcast.'

'Why?' I asked.

He said it was premature. I pointed out that work started on the project six months ago, so it could not possibly be described as premature.

'Precisely,' he said, 'rather out of date in fact.'

Remarkable! Premature *and* out-of-date?

Humphrey amended this foolishness instantly. He simply meant 'untimely', he claimed. So again, I asked him *why*?

'What I mean is, don't you think it will be rather uninteresting to the general public?' he whined.

I couldn't see why. It's an example of partnership in industry that is really happening. Now. *Extremely* interesting. I said so.

Humphrey seemed to be getting desperate. 'Quite so, Minister,' he said. 'It is *so* interesting, in fact, that there is a danger that it will obscure the main point that you wanted to make on the broadcast.'

'What is my main point?' I asked, suddenly unable to remember.

Humphrey also seemed to go blank. 'Bernard, what is the Minister's main point?'

Bernard reminded us. 'That private projects are more socially responsible with government money, and government projects are more efficient with private investment.'

This was precisely my main point. And reference to the Solihull project will obviously underline it. Humphrey really is a wet blanket. He just goes around stirring up apathy.

But he was still not satisfied. 'Minister,' he persisted. 'I must advise you very seriously with all the earnestness at my command that you do not refer to the Solihull project on the air tomorrow.'

Again I asked why? Again he dodged. But, by now, I had guessed. 'Could it be,' I enquired coldly, 'that you are planning to take all the credit for this scheme at next month's European Convention of Government Administration?'

Humphrey said, 'I beg your pardon?' – in other words, he didn't deny it! So I knew I was right. And I really tore him off a strip.

'Your keynote speech will be well reported, won't it? Well, let me explain some facts of life, Humphrey. Politicians are the ones who are ultimately responsible to the people, and it is we who get the credit. Not civil servants.'

Humphrey intervened. He assured me that he would be only too happy for me to take the credit for this project, as long as it wasn't tomorrow. Liar!

I brushed this procrastination aside. 'Humphrey,' I told him firmly, 'I am not going to fall for it. I am going to make all the political capital I can out of this Solihull project – I know a good thing when I see one.'

[*Hacker was completely mistaken. Sir Humphrey Appleby was trying to hush up all references to the Solihull project, with very good reason. Later that day Bernard Woolley, who had realised that there was more to this situation than met Hacker's eye, sought an interview with Sir Humphrey. – Ed.*]

SIR BERNARD WOOLLEY RECALLS:[1]

It was clear to me that Sir Humphrey Appleby was engaged in a cover-up of one sort or another. However, I was adamant that I needed to be fully informed about this matter, as it did not seem possible for a £74 million building project on a nine-acre site in the middle of one of our largest cities to be swept under the carpet. Even if the brush were to be wielded by Sir Humphrey Appleby.

Sir Humphrey told me that he intended to try to use the Official Secrets Act. I remarked that I couldn't see how the project could be kept secret, as it was so huge.

'It's a big secret,' replied Sir Humphrey.

I could also see no way to invoke the Official Secrets Act, when everybody knew about the project. I was young and green and had not yet fully realised that the Official Secrets Act is not to protect secrets but to protect officials.

Sir Humphrey attempted to explain his evasiveness by saying that, as the Minister had not enquired into the background of the Solihull project, he didn't wish to know. And it was, of course, standard Civil Service practice not to bother a Minister with information about which he had not enquired.

I took my courage in both hands, and indicated that I might hint to the Minister that I believed that there was a scandal connected with the Solihull project. Naturally, I made it clear to Sir Humphrey that I might *not* do so were I myself to be put more fully in the picture.

Sir Humphrey then came clean, rather reluctantly. I learned that the Solihull project had been set up by Sir Humphrey, acting for the DAA in partnership with Michael Bradley of Sloane Enterprises. This had happened long before my promotion to the Private Office.

Subsequently the Solihull Report came in, containing a paragraph casting

[1] In conversation with the Editors.

doubt on the financial soundness of Sloane Enterprises and Mr Bradley. ['*Casting doubt on the financial soundness*' *means that Bradley was probably about to go bankrupt.*' – *Ed.*]

However, by the time the Report came out, Sir Humphrey was so committed to Bradley that it seemed a better risk to him to see the project through.

Now that I knew the full facts I was in an invidious position. Naturally I could not tell the Minister something that I had learned in confidence from the Perm. Sec. Equally, I had a duty to prevent my Minister involving himself in this matter if I could. It seemed that all I could do was to remonstrate with Sir Humphrey.

I explained that if the Minister knew the full facts he would certainly not be so foolish as to broadcast them. But Sir Humphrey insisted that as a matter of principle, Ministers should never know more than they need to know. Like secret agents. Because they may be captured and tortured.

'By terrorists?' I asked.

'By the BBC,' he replied. He also explained that the situation was not lost. The bank was dithering about whether or not to foreclose – a potential disaster. He was to have lunch that week with the Bank's Chairman, Sir Desmond Glazebrook. So, meanwhile, there must be no mention of the Solihull project on the air or to the Press.

I was getting exceedingly worried about my part in what appeared to be a cover-up. I explained this to the Perm. Sec., who insisted that this was not a cover-up, it was responsible discretion exercised in the national interest to prevent unnecessary disclosure of eminently justifiable procedures in which untimely revelation would severely impair public confidence.

This sounded even worse than I thought – like Watergate! However, Sir Humphrey explained to me that Watergate was quite different. Watergate happened in America.

February 22nd

Today I did the broadcast on the Solihull project, about which I am beginning to feel a little uneasy.

I drove with BW [*Bernard Woolley – Ed.*] to BH [*Broadcasting House – Ed.*]. I asked Bernard if I had correctly diagnosed Sir Humphrey's reasons for not wanting me to mention the Solihull project on the air. This question seemed to cause Bernard considerable anguish, but he merely shook his head slowly and sadly.

So I said to him: 'What is Humphrey's real reason for not wanting me to mention it?'

Bernard opted for answering my question with a question, i.e. not answering – 'Did you not think he gave six or seven very convincing reasons, Minister?'

'No,' I said. 'Did you think that?'

He ducked that question too. 'I'm sure,' he said evasively, 'that Sir Humphrey knows what he's doing.'

Privately I agreed with this remark. I only wish that *I* knew what Sir Humphrey is doing!

I decided to approach it another way. I feel, and I don't think I'm mistaken, that Bernard has a certain sense of loyalty towards me. So I asked him what he advised me to do.

This put him into a frightful state. 'Well,' he said, panicking, 'it's not for *me* to advise, Minister, but if it were, I would be obliged to advise you that you would be well advised to follow Sir Humphrey's advice.'

'Why?' I asked.

'Well,' he dithered. 'It's just that, well, um, certain projects have certain aspects which, with sensitive handling, given reasonable discretion, when events permit, there is no *prima facie* reason why, with appropriate give and take, if all goes well, in the fullness of time, um, when the moment is ripe, um, um . . .'

'Bernard!' I interrupted him. 'You're blathering, Bernard.'

'Yes Minister,' he agreed wretchedly.

'Why are you blathering, Bernard?' I enquired.

'It's my job, Minister,' he replied, and hung his head.

Clearly he is keeping something from me. But what? Foolishly, perhaps out of spite, I resolved to talk about the project on the air and get the matter – whatever it is – out in the open.

But I now wonder if this was a mistake.

Anyway, we recorded the broadcast and I talked, at some length, with some enthusiasm, about the Solihull project.

[*We have obtained the transcript of the broadcast discussion, and reproduce overleaf the relevant pages. Those taking part were Hacker, Joe Morgan — General Secretary of the Commercial and Administrative Workers Union – and Sir George Conway, Chairman of International Construction Ltd. – Ed.*]

BBC Radio

HACKER: (CONT) and I should just like to point out that there is a perfect example of what can be done. It's going on up in Solihull now. Government money and private investment in real partnership.

MORGAN: Claptrap.

HACKER: No, no, it, um, excuse me Joe, it seems to me to be symbolic of everything this Government is working for. I've taken a great deal of personal interest in the Solihull Project.

CONWAY: Words.

HACKER: No, it's _not_ just words, it's actually there in bricks and mortar. Concrete proof, if I can use that phrase, that our policy really works in practice. And there is...

PRESENTER: Thank you Minister. One last word, Sir George?

CONWAY: I'd just like to repeat that there's nothing wrong with the principle of partnership provided, provided, that there's no interference in management decisions from the State or the work force.

PRESENTER: Thank you, Sir George. Joe Morgan?

- 3 -

BBC Radio

MORGAN: (CONT) Dear, oh dear, oh dear. We
all know that Sir George Conway is talking out-of-date capitalist
claptrap. If partnership is to mean anything at all it must mean
an equal partnership of unions, government and industry. In that
order.

PRESENTER: Minister - a final word?

HACKER: Yes, well, I think basically we're
all pretty much in agreement. Fundamentally. Aren't we? We all
realise that if only we can work together we can forge a new
Britain. And I'm delighted to have had this chance to talk about
it with two of the principal forge...principal participants.

PRESENTER: Thank you. The Right Honourable
James Hacker M.P., Minister for Administrative Affairs, was talking
with Sir George Conway, Chairman of International Construction Ltd
and Joe Morgan, General Secretary of the Commercial and Administrative
Workers Union.

- 4 -

I didn't have time to go for a drink in the Hostility Room afterwards, but as I was leaving Joe Morgan buttonholed me.

'Oh,' he said, as if spontaneously, 'I hope you don't mind me mentioning this, Mr Hacker, but I wonder if you'd be able to put in a word for my members' claim for a special Birmingham allowance?'

I naturally pointed out to him that I cannot conduct trades union negotiations in a BBC studio. Furthermore, it is a matter for the Department of Employment.

Then he made a curious remark. 'I was thinking, see,' he said, 'that after this broadcast people might start asking questions about the Solihull project, wanting to know more about it, you understand?'

'I hope they do,' I said, stubbornly. Well, I do!

Then he said. 'But, as we know . . .' and he winked, '. . . there are some things . . .' he winked again '. . . better not found out.' Then he tapped the side of his nose with his forefinger and winked again. 'I'm sure we understand each other.'

He grinned and winked again. I began to suspect that he was trying to tell me something. But what? Or – and the more probable explanation suddenly flashed into my mind – he knows something and *he thinks I know too.* But whatever it is, *I don't!*

I played for time. I watched him wink again and asked him if he had something in his eye. 'Only a gleam,' he replied cheerfully.

I must have looked awfully blank. But he must have thought I was an awfully good poker player. He continued: 'Come off it Hacker, we've got you by the short and curlies. I'm asking ten per cent below London Allowance, and we'll settle for thirty per cent below. Give you the credit for beating us down.'

'There's not going to be a Birmingham Allowance,' I said abstractedly, my mind racing. 'You'd better resign yourself to that.'

'If anyone's going to have to resign,' countered Morgan, 'it's not going to be me.'

Resign? What was the man hinting at?

'What do you mean?' I asked.

'The Solihull project, of course. I could hardly believe it when you took all the credit for it in the broadcast. Great courage of course.' Courage – how did that dreadful word get into the discussion? 'But whatever possessed you?'

I didn't know what he was on about. Cheerfully he burst into verse:

> 'Cannons to the right of him
> Cannons to the left of him.
> Into the Valley of Death rode Mr Hacker.'

I can't think what he was talking about. I'm getting very worried indeed.

[It appears that Sir Humphrey Appleby met Sir Desmond Glaze-brook for lunch at a club in Pall Mall on the same day as Hacker's broadcast. Most unusually, Sir Humphrey kept no notes and made no memos as a result of that meeting. This omission – which broke the habit and training of a lifetime in Whitehall – indicates that Sir Humphrey was profoundly frightened that the matter discussed at this meeting should ever become public knowledge.

Fortunately, however, a letter came to light many years later, sent by Sir Desmond on 23 February, the next day, to his wife who was wintering in Barbados – Ed.]

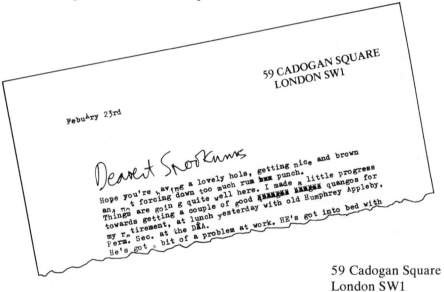

59 Cadogan Square
London SW1

Dearest Snookums [*Lady Glazebrook – Ed.*]

Hope you're having a lovely hols, getting nice and brown and not forcing down too much rum punch.

Things are going quite well here. I made a little progress towards getting a couple of good quangos for my retirement, at lunch yesterday with old Humphrey Appleby, Perm. Sec. at the DAA [QUANGO – *an acronym for Quasi Autonomous Non Government Organisation – Ed.*]

He's got a bit of a problem at work. He's got into bed with some idiot whizz kid financier called Bradley, on a building project in Solihull. It seems that the whizz kid has taken the money and run, leaving old Humphrey holding the bag. Anyway, I couldn't follow all the details because I'd had rather too much of the claret but, to cut a long story short, as Bradley can't

155

pay his bills Humphrey wants our bank to take over the contract. He promised me that HMG would turn it all into a successful and profitable venture and all that bullshit. Whoever heard of the government being involved in a successful and profitable venture? Does he think I was born yesterday?

Naturally, I'd be perfectly happy to help good old Humph. out of a jam – it can't cost me anything, of course, since I'm retiring next year. But I told him that it's up to the Board and it could go either way. He swallowed that, I think, or pretended to anyway. I naturally chose that moment to remark that I was hoping to hear news of the new Ministry Co-Partnership Commission. I'm after the Chairmanship – £8000 a year part-time just the thing to boost my meagre pension, don't you think, Snookums?

To my astonishment he told me that my name was on a *shortlist* for a couple of quangos. Shortlist, mark you! Bloody insult. Quangos can't suddenly be in short supply, no government ever cuts quangos without instantly replacing them with others. [*At this time there were about 8000 paid appointments within the gift of Ministers to Quangos, at a cost to the taxpayer of £5 million per year. – Ed.*]

Humphrey, of course, pretended it was difficult to find me a quango, rather as I'd pretended that it was difficult for the bank to find his money.

He went through the most extraordinary routine. He mentioned the Advisory Committee of Dental Establishments, and asked if I knew anything about teeth. I pointed out that I was a banker. As I knew nothing about teeth, he then ruled out the Milk Marketing Board. Can't quite see the connection myself.

He offered the Dumping at Sea Representations Panel, asking if I lived near the sea. I asked if Knightsbridge was near enough – but apparently not. So it seems I'm out of the running for the Clyde River Purification Board too.

Then, with every bit of the meal, Humphrey had a new idea. Rump steak suggested to him the Meat Marketing Board; but I don't know a damn thing about meat. The fact that I eat it is not quite a close enough connection. So the Meat and Livestock Commission was ruled out too. *I'd* ordered Dover Sole, it reminded H. of the White Fish Authority. And, as the veg. arrived, he suggested the Potato Marketing Board, the Governors of the National Vegetable Research Station, the National Biological Standards Board, or the Arable Crops and Forage Board.

With the wine he suggested the Food and Drink Training Board. When I asked for mustard he mentioned the Food Additives and Contaminants Committee, and when we saw a Steak Diane being flambéed at the next table he offered the Fire Services Examination Board, the British Safety Council, and the St John's Ambulance.

Of course, all of this was to make his point that he too was demanding a *quid pro quo*. But it was rather humiliating because after all this he asked me rather querulously: if I knew nothing about *any* of these quangos, what *did* I know about? I was forced to explain that there was nothing I knew about particularly – after all, I'm a banker. It's not required.

Then he asked me if there were any minority groups that I could represent. I suggested bankers. After all, there aren't very many of us. He didn't seem to think that was the answer.

He explained to me that the ideal quango appointee is a black, Welsh, disabled woman trades unionist. He asked me if I knew one of them, but I don't.

I remarked that women are not a minority group and nor are trades unionists. Humphrey agreed, but explained that they share the same paranoia which is, after all, the distinguishing feature of any minority group.

So at the end of this whole rigmarole, he was basically saying that my quango chances boil down to his Ministry's Industry Co-Partnership Commission, the Chairmanship of which is within the gift of his Minister.

It sounds ideal, actually. There's lots of papers but Old Humph. made it quite clear that it's not awfully necessary to read them; that, in fact he'd be delighted if I didn't bother so that I wouldn't have too much to say at the monthly meetings.

So it looks like we'll be scratching each other's backs. I'll have a word with my board, he'll have a word with his Minister, and I'll see you on the beach next week.

Your loving
Desi-pooh.

February 23rd

Had a very worrying conversation with Roy, my driver, today. Didn't see him after recording the broadcast yesterday, because I was given a relief driver.

Roy asked me how the recording went. I said it had gone very well, that I'd talked about government partnership with industry, and that there was a most interesting project going on up in the Midlands.

I assumed he wouldn't have heard of it. I was wrong.

'You don't mean the Solihull project, sir?'

I was astonished. 'Yes,' I said. 'You've heard of it.'

Roy chuckled.

I waited, but he said nothing. 'What are you laughing at?' I asked.

'Nothing, sir,' he said. Then he chuckled again.

He'd obviously heard something.

'What have you heard?' I asked.

'Nothing. Really.'

I could see his face in the rear-view mirror. He was smiling. I didn't like it.

He was obviously laughing at some aspect of the Solihull project. But what? For some reason, I felt a need to defend it. To my *driver*? I must be cracking up. But I said, 'We regard it as a shining example of a successful collaboration between government and private enterprise.'

Roy chuckled again. He was really getting on my nerves.

'Roy, what's so funny?' I demanded. 'What do you know about all this?'

'No more than you might pick up on about thirty journeys between the DAA and Mr Michael Bradley's Office, 44 Farringdon Street, and 129 Birmingham Road, Solihull,' he replied.

'Thirty journeys?' I was astonished. 'Who with?'

'Oh,' said Roy cheerfully, 'your predecessor, sir, and Sir Humphrey, mostly.' He chuckled again. I could have killed him. What's so bloody funny, I'd like to know? 'Very cheerful they were on the first few trips. They kept talking about shining examples of successful collaboration and suchlike. Then . . .', he paused for effect, '. . . then the gloom started to come down, if you know what I mean, sir?'

Gloom? What did he mean, gloom? 'Gloom?'

'Well, no, not gloom, exactly,' said Roy and I relaxed momentarily. 'More like desperation really.' Oh my God!

My own mood was also moving inexorably from gloom to desperation. 'Desperation?' I asked desperately.

'Well,' said George. 'You're the one who knows the background, aren't you, sir?'

I nodded. 'Yes I am.' I suppose I must have been a trifle unconvincing because my damn driver chuckled again.

'Was there . . . um . . . any . . . er . . . any particular bit of the background you were thinking of?' I tried to ask in a casual sort of way, still in a state of total mental chaos.

'No,' Roy said firmly. 'I mean, when something's fishy, it's just fishy isn't it? You don't know which particular bit the smell's coming from.'

'Fishy?' Did he know more than he was letting on? *What's* fishy?

'Well,' continued Roy helpfully, 'I mean, I don't really know do I? For all I know Mr Bradley may be quite kosher, despite everything Sir Humphrey said about him. Still, you'd know more about all that than I do, sir. I'm just the driver.'

Yes, I thought bitterly. What do I know? I'm just the bloody Minister.

February 25th

I've spent the weekend wondering if I can get any more information out of Roy. Does he know more, or has he told me everything he knows? Perhaps he can find out more, on the driver's network. Information is currency among the drivers. They leak all over the place. On the other hand, perhaps he'll trade the information that *I* don't know anything at all about the Solihull project – which could be very damaging to me, couldn't it?

But the question is, how to find out if Roy knows any more without losing face myself. (Or losing any *more* face.) I've heard that drivers can be silenced with an MBE – can I get more information with the hint or promise of an MBE? But how would I drop the hint?

These are foolish and desperate thoughts. First I'll try and get the truth out of my Permanent Secretary. Then I'll try my Private Secretary. Only then will I turn to my driver.

It occurs to me, thinking generally around the problems that I've encountered in the last six months, that it is not possible to be a good Minister so long as the Civil Service is allowed complete control over its own recruitment. Perhaps it *is* impossible to stop the Civil Service appointing people in its own likeness, but we politicians ought to try to stop it growing like Frankenstein.

This whole matter of the Solihull project – which I am determined to get to the bottom of – has reminded me how incomplete is my picture of my Department's activities. We politicians hardly ever know if information is being concealed, because the concealment is concealed too. We are only offered a choice of options, *all* of which are acceptable to the permanent officials, and, in any case, they force decisions on us the way magicians force cards on their audience in the Three Card Trick. 'Choose any card, choose my card.' But somehow we always choose the card they want us to choose. And how is it managed that we never seem to choose a course of action that the Civil Service doesn't approve? Because we're too busy to draft any of the documents ourselves, and he who drafts the document wins the day.

In fact, the more I think about it, the more the Department appears to be an iceberg, with nine-tenths of it below the surface, invisible, unknown, and deeply dangerous. And I am forced to spend my life manicuring the tip of this iceberg.

My Department has a great purpose – to bring administration, bureaucracy and red tape under control. Yet everything that my officials do ensures that not only does the DAA not achieve its purpose, but that it achieves the opposite.

Unfortunately, most government departments achieve the opposite of their purpose: the Commonwealth Office lost us the Commonwealth, the Department of Industry reduces industry, the Department of Transport presided over the disintegration of our public transport systems, the Treasury loses our money – I could go on for ever.

And their greatest skill of all is the low profile. These so-called servants of ours are immune from the facts of life. The ordinary rules of living don't apply to civil servants: they don't suffer from inflation, they don't suffer from unemployment, they automatically get honours.

Jobs are never lost – the only cuts are in planned recruitment. I have found out that there were just two exemptions to the 1975 policy of a mandatory five per cent incomes policy – annual increments and professional fees: annual increments because that is how civil servants get pay rises, and professional fees on the insistence of parliamentary Counsel, the lawyers who drafted the legislation. Otherwise the legislation would never have been drafted!

So what have I learned after nearly six months in office? Merely, it seems, that I am almost impotent in the face of the mighty faceless bureaucracy. However, it is excellent that I realise this because it means that they have failed to housetrain me. If I were housetrained I would now believe a) that I am immensely powerful, and b) that my officials merely do my bidding.

So there is hope. And I am resolved that I shall not leave my office tomorrow until I have got right to the bottom of this strange mystery surrounding the Solihull project. There must be *some* way of finding out what's going on.

February 26th
Today was a real eye-opener.

I hadn't seen Sir Humphrey for some days. We met, at my request, to discuss the Solihull project. I explained that I had talked rather enthusiastically about the project on the air, but I am now having second thoughts.

'Any particular reason?' asked Sir Humphrey politely.

I didn't beat about the bush. 'Humphrey,' I said, 'is everything all right with the Solihull project?'

'I believe the building works are proceeding quite satisfactorily, Minister,' he replied smoothly.

160

I patiently explained that that was not quite what I meant. 'What is going on?' I asked.

'Building is going on, Minister,' he reported.

'Yes,' I said trying to keep my temper, 'but . . . something is up, isn't it?'

'Yes indeed,' he replied. At last I'm getting somewhere, I thought. I relaxed.

'What is up?' I said.

'The first floor is up,' said Sir Humphrey, 'and the second is almost up.'

I began to show my annoyance. 'Humphrey, please! I'm talking about the whole basis of the project.'

'Ah,' replied my Perm. Sec. gravely. 'I see.'

'What can you tell me about that?'

'Well, as I understand it, Minister . . .' here it comes, I thought, the truth at last, '. . . the basis is an aggregate of gravel and cement on six feet of best builder's rubble.'

Does he take me for a complete fool?

'Humphrey,' I said sternly, 'I think you know I am talking about the finance.'

So then he rabbited on about our contract with the construction company, and the usual stage payments, and all sorts of useless rubbish. I interrupted him.

'What is it,' I demanded, 'that I don't know?'

'What do you mean, precisely?' was his evasive reply.

In a state of mounting hysteria, I tried to explain. 'I don't know. It's just that . . . there's something I don't know, and I don't know because I can't find the right question to ask you because I don't know what to ask. What is it that I don't know?'

Sir Humphrey feigned innocence.

'Minister,' he said, '*I* don't know what you don't know. It could be almost anything.'

'But,' I persisted, 'you are keeping things from me, aren't you?'
He nodded.

'*What*?' I was nearly at boiling point by now. He smiled patronisingly at me. It was quite intolerable. He explained that it is the Department's duty to protect the Minister from the great tide of irrelevant information that beats against the walls of the Department day after day.

This was not the answer I was seeking. I stood up, and made one last attempt at explaining my problem – just in case he didn't fully understand it. 'Look Humphrey,' I began, 'there is something about the Solihull project that I know I don't know, and I know *you* know. I know *Bernard* knows. *Joe Morgan* knows. For heaven's sake, even my *driver* knows. It's only poor old Joe Soap here who has to stand up and talk about it in front of the British people who hasn't got a clue what's going on.'

Humphrey just stared at me. He said nothing. So I tried to spell it out for him.

'Humphrey,' I said, resisting the temptation to tear out my hair. Or his hair. 'Will you please answer one simple question?'

'Certainly Minister,' he said. 'What is it?'

'*I don't know*!' I yelled. 'You tell me and I'll ask it!'

February 28th

Today seemed to last an eternity. Ruin stared me in the face.

It began with another meeting with Humphrey. The atmosphere was distinctly frosty – Frank Weisel was there too, wanting to discuss his new paper about quangos.

I wasn't a bit interested in discussing quangos today, which seem to have no immediate relevance to my current problems, though it was full of stuff about 'ending the scandal of ministerial patronage' and 'jobs for the boys'. Humphrey described it as 'most imaginative' which Frank interpreted as a sign of approval. Frank hasn't yet learned that 'original' and 'imaginative' are two of Humphrey's most damning criticisms.

Frank's scheme was to hand over all quango appointments to a select committee of Parliament. 'Get the best men for the jobs instead of old chums, party hacks, and you scratch my back and I'll scratch yours,' he explained with his usual charm.

It seemed to me that it was a good plan, and I suggested we put it forward for legislation.

'It's certainly a novel proposal,' remarked Humphrey. 'Novel' – that's the other killer!

But Humphrey went on to explain his view that there was no sense in upsetting the current system when it is working smoothly.

Smoothly? I'd never heard such nonsense. Only this morning I'd received a proposal for the Chairmanship of the new Industrial Co-partnership Commission, the latest quango. And whose name was being put up? Sir Desmond Glazebrook, of all people. 'He's never worked in industry,' I said to Humphrey, 'he's never met a trades unionist, and he's said a whole lot of nasty things about this government – is this the kind of suggestion a smoothly working system comes up with?'

'But he would be an excellent Chairman,' said Sir Humphrey.

'He's an ignorant buffoon,' I explained carefully.

'Nonetheless,' said Sir Humphrey, 'an excellent Chairman.'

I told Humphrey that I drew the line at Glazebrook. I absolutely refused to appoint him. Over my dead body, I declared.

There was silence in the office for some moments. Then Sir Humphrey said, 'Minister, before you make your *final* decision I think there is something that you ought to see.'

And he produced a Ministry file. On the cover was written SOLIHULL PROJECT – TOP SECRET. Why top secret? I opened it. I saw why. Bradley, our Department's partner, owed £7½ million, was going bankrupt, and the entire project was in imminent danger of collapse.

I was aghast. Absolutely aghast. I asked Humphrey why I hadn't been told any of this and he wittered on idiotically about how he was deeply conscious of the heavy burdens of my office. It seems to me that he's made them quite a lot heavier in the last few days.

'If this comes out,' I said weakly, 'it will be all over the front pages. A public scandal. A disaster.'

'Appalling,' added Bernard. He's always such a comfort!

Then for a moment, Frank gave me a tiny ray of hope. 'Hold on Jim.' He grabbed the file. 'Look, this report is dated before the election. You're in the clear.'

'Unfortunately,' murmured Humphrey, 'under the convention of Ministerial responsibility, the blame must fall . . .'

Frank interrupted him. 'But everyone will know it wasn't Jim.'

'Quite so.' Sir Humphrey shook his head mournfully. 'But the principle of democratic accountability requires the occasional human sacrifice – Crichel Down and all that.[1] When the pack is baying for blood . . . isn't that so, Minister?'

I couldn't speak.

[1] The Crichel Down affair in 1954 was possibly the last example of a Minister accepting full responsibility for a scandal within his Department, about which he did not know and could not have known. Nevertheless, Sir Thomas Dugdale, then Minister of Agriculture and Fisheries, accepted that as the Minister he was constitutionally responsible to Parliament for the wrong actions of his officials, even though their actions were not ordered by him and would not have been approved by him. He resigned, was kicked upstairs to the Lords and a promising career came to an end. No Minister since then has been – depending on your point of view – either so scrupulous or so foolish.

Frank was undeterred. 'Surely he has only to point to the dates?'

'Ah, well,' Sir Humphrey put on his most pious expression, 'a lesser man might try to wriggle out of it. But there is only one honourable course. As the Minister is well aware.' He gazed at me sorrowfully and shook his head again. I felt I was at my own funeral.

'Don't you think Frank might have a point?' I asked, determined to fight to the last.

'Yes,' said Bernard, 'except that in that broadcast, which goes out . . .'

'Today,' I interjected.

'. . . Today,' continued Bernard,' you publicly identified yourself with the success of the project. In fact, it'll be on the air any minute now.'

We all gaped at each other. Then Bernard rushed for the radio.

I shouted, 'Bernard, get on to the BBC and stop it.'

Humphrey said, 'I wish you luck Minister, but – well, you know what the BBC are like.'

'Yes,' I agreed, 'but surely in a case like this, a crisis, an emergency, a scandal . . .'

'Yes,' he nodded, 'if you put it like that, they might move it to peak listening time. And then repeat it. And film it for *Panorama*.'

'I'll order them to cancel it,' I said.

'MINISTER TRIES TO CENSOR BBC,' said Humphrey, gloomily dreaming up headlines again.

I could see his point, of course. It was obviously hopeless. I was just about to suggest asking them very, very nicely when Bernard hurried in holding a transistor, and out of it came my voice saying all those dreadful things about Government money and private investment in a real partnership, and how I took such a great personal interest in the Solihull project and how it is symbolic of everything this government is working for – concrete proof that our policy really works in practice.

I switched it off. I couldn't bear to listen to it. We gazed at each other, bleakly, in silence.

I waited. Nobody spoke.

Eventually I did.

'Humphrey,' I asked quietly, 'why did you let me say all that?'

'Minister,' he assumed his I'm-just-a-humble-civil-servant manner, 'I can only advise. I did advise. I advised most strongly. But when an adviser's advice is unheeded . . .'

He petered out, only too aware that he'd kept some rather vital information back from me.

'Advise me now,' I said coldly.

'Certainly Minister.' He thought for a moment. 'Now, it is possible Bartletts Bank will take over from Sloane Enterprises, and all will be well.'

The bank! I'd never thought of that. It seemed too good to be true!

'But . . .' said Humphrey.

Clearly it *was* too good to be true.

'But . . . the bank is hesitant. However, the Director in charge is retiring next year and is anxious for some appointment. The Chairmanship of a quango, for instance.'

I could see no problem at all. 'Give him one,' I said immediately. 'Give him that one you were proposing that fool Desmond Glazebrook for. Who is the Director in charge, anyway?'

'Desmond Glazebrook,' explained Humphrey. And suddenly it all became clear.

I felt I had to leave a decent pause before I said that actually he's not such a bad chap really.

Frank was extraordinarily slow on the uptake. 'He's always attacking the government,' he said angrily.

I explained to Frank that it does us good to appoint our opponents occasionally. It's democratic – statesmanlike.

Frank seemed unimpressed with this point of view, and he argued and argued till finally I just told him to shut up.

I asked Humphrey who else knew about this wretched Solihull report. Only Joe Morgan, Humphrey told me – which suddenly explained his confident claim for a Birmingham Allowance. Blackmail!

And it occurred to me at that moment that Desmond Glazebrook might need a *Deputy* Chairman, one with real experience of industry. A trades unionist, perhaps. I mentioned it to Humphrey, who thought it was an awfully good idea, and he immediately suggested Joe Morgan. *I* thought *that* was an awfully good idea.

'It takes two to quango, Minister,' smiled Humphrey, and we got them both on the phone right away.

Frank watched us in silence, and when we'd had brief chats with Desmond and Joe he had an absolutely amazing outburst – 'This is exactly what I've been talking about', he shouted, even louder than usual. 'This is what's wrong with the system. Jobs for the boys. *Quid pro quo*. Corruption.' I couldn't believe my ears, Frank accusing *me* of corruption. What an idea! He's obviously going off his rocker.

'What about my quango abolition paper?' he yelled, going red in the face.

'Very good Frank,' I said smoothly. 'Imaginative. Ingenious.'

'Novel,' added Humphrey.

Then Frank announced that he wouldn't let me suppress it. As if I would do such a thing! Me, suppress papers? I'm a democrat, a believer in open government. Frank must be raving mad.

'I'll get it to Cabinet through someone else,' he threatened at the top of his not inconsiderable voice. 'I'll get it adopted as party policy. You'll see.'

He marched to the door. Then he stopped, and turned. He had a beatific smile on his face. I didn't like the look of it one bit. Whenever Frank smiles you know that something very nasty is about to happen. 'The Press,' he said softly. 'The Press. If the Press were to get hold of this . . .'

And suddenly, I had a brainwave. 'Frank,' I said gently, 'I've been thinking. Changing the subject completely, of course, but have *you* ever thought about serving on a quango?'

'Oh no,' he replied, smiling his most unpleasant smile, 'you're not corrupting me!'

I explained patiently that nothing could be further from my thoughts. My idea is that, even better than abolishing the quango system, would be to make it work. And that if we set up a commission to supervise and report on the composition and activities of all quangos, it could be the answer. It could have very senior people, most Privy Councillors. I know that Frank has always secretly fancied himself hob-nobbing with Privy Councillors. I explained that such a body would need some really able people, people who have studied quangos, people who know the abuses of the system. 'And in view of your knowledge, and concern,' I finished, 'Humphrey suggested your name.'

'Privy Councillors?' said Frank, hypnotised.

'It's up to you, of course,' I added, 'but it would be a great service to the public. How do you feel?'

'You're not going to change my opinions, you know,' said Frank thoughtfully. 'There is such a thing as integrity.'

Humphrey and I both hastened to agree with Frank on the importance of integrity, and we pointed out that it was, in fact, his very integrity that would make him such a good member of this quango.

'Mind you,' Humphrey said, instinctively aware of Frank's enormous sense of guilt which needs constant absolution and aware also of his deep commitment to the puritan work ethic, 'it would be very hard work. I'm sure that service in this super-quango would involve a great deal of arduous foreign travel, to see how they manage these matters in other important government centres – Japan, Australia, California, the West Indies . . .

'Tahiti,' I added helpfully.

'Tahiti,' agreed Sir Humphrey.

'Yes,' said Frank with an expression of acute suffering on his face, 'it would be arduous, wouldn't it?'

'Very arduous,' we both said. Several times.

'But serving the public's what it's all about, isn't it?' asked Frank hopefully.

Humphrey and I murmured, 'serving the public, exactly' once or twice.

Then Frank said, 'And what about my quango paper?'

I told him it would be invaluable, and that he should take it with him.

And Humphrey offered to keep a copy on the files – with the Solihull Report